DEATH BY DISH

CLAIRE HARLOW

CONTENTS

1

— · —

UNDER THE WARM EMBRACE of a sunlit sky, the long-awaited Sparrow Haven Tides and Tastings Fair was underway in my quaint village, located in the heart of New England. A palpable buzz of excitement permeated the humid summer air, mingling with the tantalizing aromas wafting from the assortment of stalls and stands spotting the festive landscape. Vibrant umbrellas cast dappled shadows over bustling chefs as they made finishing touches to their culinary masterpieces.

Amidst the festivities, the mesmerizing whirl of fair rides added a whimsical dimension to my surroundings. The laughter of children and exhilarated screams of thrill-seekers intermingled with the scents of cotton candy and popcorn. In the distance, a vibrant, revolving Ferris wheel offered its riders a panoramic view of the fairgrounds.

Sweet Barkley and I were headed to the Ferris wheel now to meet my boyfriend, Ethan. Out of the two of us, I wasn't sure who was more excited about seeing Ethan after being apart for a week. Judging by my dog's non-stop waving tail, I'd say it was a tie. I had taken a full week off from my job at the library with three activities in mind: my boyfriend, my bestie, and the fair.

Ethan and I spotted one another at the same time as he was turning around. He held two clear cups of lemonade. His straight, white smile made my heart skip a beat.

After handing me one of the cups, Ethan embraced me before bending down to give Barkley some love. "Oh, it's good to be back. I'm glad to see you too, sweet boy." He straightened and pecked my cheek. "I missed you, beautiful."

"We missed you too. How was the conference?"

He blew a dark curl from his forehead. "Good. Very informative. What would you like to know about repairing anterior cruciate ligaments in fur-babies?"

I made a sour face. "Not at all but thanks for offering."

He chuckled and glanced around. "Did your bestie plan on meeting us here as well?"

"No, Milly is actually part of the tasting fair. She's playing chef at the clam chowder table as we speak."

His brow rose. "A chef? I thought you said she could burn water."

"Usually, but she's got one specialty. The girl makes one mean miso paste."

"What in the world is miso paste?" he asked before taking a swig of his drink.

I took his hand, and we headed to the tasting tables. The fair planners had scheduled the event to start at eleven thirty, which was now in fifteen minutes.

"I ferment miso soybean paste. She combines soybeans, salt, and koji. And before you ask, koji is a fungus. She made the concoction months ago for, in her words, 'ample fermentation.'"

It was his turn to make a sour face. "Uh, sorry I asked. You look good in those shorts, by the way. A tan suits you."

I glanced down at my long, slender legs. "A tan suits everybody. But I'm glad you approve," I said, sending him a wink.

Anticipation rising, we continued down the dirt path, navigating our way through a throng of fellow food enthusiasts, with Barkley trotting along my side as his eyes darted in every direction.

My gaze, like a compass drawn to true north, fixed on the epicenter of this unfolding event: the legendary clam chowder station. A communal hush seemed to settle over the fairground as Victoria Thorne, the esteemed judge, approached, her very presence a solemn benediction to the culinary artistry awaiting her judgement.

We were fortunate enough to make it to the front of the growing crowd. Spotting Milly behind the table, I waved and sent her a thumbs up. She smiled and made a silent clapping motion with bright pink polished fingernails, sure to glow in the dark.

The chowder, a cauldron of maritime secrets and heritage, bubbled under the steam as Victoria dipped her spoon into its creamy depth. The velvety liquid clung to the utensil like a silken embrace. Victoria's lips met the spoon with a delicate grace, and time itself seemed to pause, hanging on the precipice of her verdict.

A subtle shift in her expression, unreadable to all but the most observant, signaled at her judgement. Her eyes, like twin beacons of discernment, grew wide at the culmination of a culinary legacy that spanned generations. Finally, a smile of contented approval curved her lips.

A collective exhale rippled through the crowd in joint relief. As the crowd cheered, she had a word with the head chef for several moments.

Victoria's fingers, which usually danced with grace across her notebook, trembled slightly as she attempted to jot down her impressions of the chowder. Her once-confidant demeanor now bore a subtle strain of discomfort.

Something was off. I felt it in my gut, and the feeling caused a knot to form in my stomach.

Glancing down at her notebook opened on the table, her words held a jittery quality, her typical neatness giving way to erratic loops and jagged lines. A thin sheen of sweat glistened on her brow and upper-lip, and her face shifted between ashen and flushed. Victoria dabbed at her face with a napkin, her movements betraying the effort it was taking her to maintain a semblance of normalcy. She cleared her throat, her voice faltering as she engaged in conversation with the head chef again. Then she gripped the edge of the table, her knuckles turning white as she attempted to steady herself.

Murmurs rose through the crowd who watched as Chef Antonio helped Victoria to a seat behind the table. Milly placed a cup of water before her and knelt down to say something in a hushed tone.

With a polite excuse, Victoria rose from her seat, her legs protesting with a subtle wobble as she clutched a fisted hand to her chest. With wide, glassy eyes, the sickly woman glanced back at the pot of chowder before collapsing into a heap on the grass.

Milly and the others at the table rushed over to her.

Victoria's breath was shallow. "I can't move," she cried, as her breathing became labored.

Milly covered her mouth and screamed, "Call 911!" She checked Victoria's neck for a pulse before darting a look to Ethan who ran over to the group. "I can't find a pulse. Ethan. Please," she cried out.

Ethan knelt down to check as well before shaking his head. A female medic in the crowd came forward to help Ethan try to resuscitate her but to no avail.

The horrified faces in the crowd seemed to reflect my sick stomach as I sent my close friend, Detective Fred O'Malley, an urgent text with our location. He was on duty here at the fair today, so he'd likely appear within minutes.

Parents guided their children away while others stayed, cries and sniffles rising all around us.

Once Fred was on the scene, he made the crowd disperse, and his team taped off the area as the paramedics took the covered body of Victoria Thorne away. Within two hours, the fair workers had all the rides shut down, and the fair was closed, set to be reopened to the public in the morning.

Once the officers collected the utensils and pot of chowder into evidence, Antonio, Nancy, and Milly began talking to Fred all at once. They tried explaining the nightmare of a scene everyone had just witnessed.

Fred raised his hand. "Whoa, just calm down. Milly, why don't you walk me through everything, and then if anyone wants to add anything afterward, they can."

My throat tightened as I listened to my best friend replay the tasting in a shaky voice, tears streaming down her face from beginning to end.

Antonio crossed his arms. "Victoria's death had nothing to do with the chowder, detective. Surely you know this. She does the tasting every year and has had no adverse effects from clams or anything else."

"Yes," Nancy agreed. "She must have had a heart attack. You saw the way she clutched her chest before falling to the ground. Right, Ms. Harper?" she asked, turning to me.

As the local sleuth for several years now, this didn't surprise me. "Yes, she did. And nobody is accusing any of you of anything. Fred is just following protocol."

Fred nodded. "That's right. But since I have the three of you here, I'm going to ask a few questions since the timing of death took place so closely to her consuming the chowder."

Antonio's face warmed to crimson. "This is absurd."

"It's utterly ridiculous and a waste of our time, is what it is," Nancy chimed in.

Fred hiked up his pants a notch before placing his hands on his belt. "I'm not interested in opinions. Just information. Got it?" he asked, glancing from Antonio to Nancy.

They remained silent with disapproving looks on their faces as they both nodded.

Fred pulled a pen from his shirt pocket and opened a spiral-bound notebook. "Did any of you taste the chowder in the pot used for the tasting today? You know, for flavor or whatnot?"

They all said no in unison.

Then Milly explained. "We cooked the chowder yesterday in a much larger pot. That's when we tasted and perfected the flavor. Then we poured a portion of the chowder into the one pot for today's tasting. The flavors marry overnight, you see. And the rest was going to be sold to the fair attendees."

"Where did the tasting pot stay during the night?" he asked, jotting something down.

Milly rapidly blinked. "At my house. I added a little additional miso paste this morning to give it a more fresher, more robust flavor." She shook her head. "But I used the same batch of miso from the day before...the same one we all sampled. I didn't tamper with the paste at all this morning."

Fred drug his fingers downward on his mustache.

I fought the urge to vomit, my mouth filling with bile. The sour liquid burned my throat as I swallowed against the urge. If the autopsy or chowder came back positive for poison, my best friend would become the prime suspect in a murder investigation. Surely, any moment now, I'd wake up from this nightmare.

Ethan placed a protective, strong arm around my waist and drew me closer.

"Did Mrs. Thorne do any tastings prior to the chowder?" Fred asked.

"No," Nancy answered. "And I know for a fact she fasts and only drinks water the morning before tastings. She says...she used to say it was for a clean palate and a healthy appetite."

Fred nodded. "Where is Mrs. Thorne from?"

"Ballentine. You know, the town about an hour from here?"

"Did she plan to stay after today?"

Nancy sighed. "She had five days of various tastings around town. I don't know if she made reservations or if she planned to drive back and forth each day."

"Did her husband or anyone else come with her?"

Antonio piped in. "Yes, but not for the fair. Her husband came to do some deep-sea fishing. This will crush the poor man. I can't imagine losing my wife."

"How old was Mrs. Thorne?" Fred asked.

Antonio and Nancy shrugged. "Early seventies maybe?"

"She was in her sixties," Milly corrected. "Victoria turned sixty-eight last month."

"Alright, there's no reason to hold you all up any longer. I appreciate your time and cooperation. And Nancy, you're likely correct to assume Mrs. Thorne had something internally occur. If so, we'll know soon. Very sad, indeed."

Antonio and Nancy agreed and hurried away toward the fair's exit.

Fred squeezed Milly's arm. "You don't need to worry yourself, Milly. Regardless of what we find out, you know I have your back." He sent Ethan and me a thoughtful smile. "I'll be in touch, kiddo."

"Yeah, thanks, Fred," I said.

Milly threw herself into my opened arms and had a good cry.

"Why don't you stay the night at my house, Milly? You know Barkley is the best comforter ever. You'll sleep better with him snuggled up to you."

She reached down to give Barkley a kiss. "You better believe I'm spending the night. Do you really think Victoria had a stroke or something?"

"Yeah, for sure. You have nothing to worry about, bestie."

2

—.—

I WAS RELIEVED THAT Milly had taken off from work with me as well. Whether Victoria's death was by her creator's design, or someone had poisoned her, it had left Milly badly shaken up. Mr. and Mrs. Thorne had been close friends with Milly and her parents for many years.

Milly's mother, Mary Johnson, worked as a talented seamstress out of her home, and Victoria loved to sew. The two ladies got together at least once a month to share new ideas and work on sewing projects together. Milly's dad, Charles, worked as a local fisherman. He and Victoria's husband had been out deep-sea fishing together when his wife's death had occurred.

My bestie had a close-knit family, and I'd known them my whole life. They were loving, supportive, and hard-working people, who I respected a lot. Her parents' dedication to their crafts and their love for the village had inspired Milly's own passion for art and community.

So, when Milly woke late the morning after the fatal tasting, I offered to take her home to pack and then take her to her parents' home, so she could be with them during this difficult time.

Nestled along the rugged coastline, Milly's childhood home sat as a quaint retreat, where tales of a fisherman's adventure mingled with the delicate stories of creating fabric delights.

The exterior of their house exuded a rustic charm that harmonized effortlessly with its rugged surroundings. A weathered shingle façade showcased years of enduring New England's coastal elements, while windows framed in soft white paint peered out onto the expanse of the sea. Colorful buoys and fishing nets hung as decorative accents, paying homage to Charles's maritime trade.

The interior was a relaxing haven where knitted blankets adorned worn-in armchairs. The walls boasted a collection of nautical relics and lovely hand-sewn tapestries. Antique bookshelves, stacked full to entertain any reader's genre of taste, lined the main room.

We found Mary upstairs in a cozy attic that they had transformed into a sewing sanctuary. Sunlight filtered through the lace curtains, casting a soft glow upon spools of thread and carefully arranged fabrics.

The gentle hum of a sewing machine halted as Milly and I entered the room. Mary stood and rushed over to give an extended hug to both of us.

Milly looked so much like her mother. They had the same sparkling blue eyes and straight, auburn hair, though her mother's was mixed with silver around her face now. Milly had been lucky enough to get her mother's curvy figure as well.

Mary dabbed at a falling tear. "I just can't believe it. Victoria was standing in this very room the day before yesterday." She cupped Milly's face and kissed her cheek before glancing over to me. "Olivia, sweetie, have you heard from Fred?"

I squeezed her hand. "I might know something by this evening at the soonest. But it may be longer. Maybe even days."

With slumped shoulders, Mary motioned for us to follow. "Come on. I could use a cup of coffee. How about you two?"

We both said yes at the same time.

"And Milly needs to eat something," I added. "She hasn't had a bite since yesterday morning."

Sticking her tongue out, Milly swatted at my backside.

Mary turned and gave her daughter a stern look. "Amelia Johnson. I know this is difficult, but you need to take care of yourself. You can't afford to lose any weight, darling."

"I disagree with you there, but okay, Mom."

Mary poured coffee grinds into a filter before filling the pot with water. "Are you seeing anyone, darling?"

I knew Mary well enough to know she was trying to help get everyone's mind off of Victoria for the time being.

Milly rolled her eyes. "I'm on vacation from work *and* men."

Mary set a bowl of cantaloupe, blueberries, and strawberries on the table and then opened a canister of granola. She pointed to us both. "Eat, you two. It's light, so I don't want to hear any back talk." She poured us each a cup of coffee and took a seat across from us. "What about...oh, what was his name, dear? Roger?"

Milly shuddered. "His name is now slobber. Kissing Roger was like kissing a Saint Bernard. So gross."

Mary put her hand to her mouth. "Oh dear, don't make me spit coffee all over the place." She patted Milly's hand. "One day, you'll find your soulmate. Just like Olivia has," she added with a wink to me.

It was my turn to cover my mouth. "Uh, I don't believe in the whole soulmate idea. But I'm very happy, and Ethan really is a great guy."

Milly snorted. "A great guy? A great guy puts the toilet seat back down. Ethan is near perfect. And you're perfect for him, too. If that's not the definition of soulmates, I don't know what is." Her voice rose an octave. "And he's stupid hot."

Mary smiled. "Ethan is handsome, and he's an amazing vet. Mittens just loves him."

"Speaking of Mittens, where is she? And where is Dad? Fishing?"

She glanced toward the kitchen window. "Mittens is hiding some-where. She's grown ornery in her old age. Your dad is with Richard. He...went to help him plan...you know," Mary put her face in her hands. "Oh, I'm sorry."

Milly started crying too, making my throat tighten.

"I'm so sorry for your family's loss. That was good of Charles to go with him," I said. "Did Mrs. Thorne have any medical conditions, Mary?" I cleared my throat. "Or if you don't feel like talking—"

"It's fine, sweetie. We can't keep pretending like nothing happened. Yeah, she had diabetes, but she kept it in check and was healthy oth-erwise."

"Nancy said that she was fasting before the tasting. Isn't that dan-gerous for a diabetic?"

Mary shook her head. "Victoria never skipped a meal in her life. I don't know why she made stuff up so often. Not to us, but to other people. One time, when we were shopping at a fabric store, she told the clerk that her son was an NFL player." She shook her head. "But after they lost their first and only child to leukemia, they never wanted any more children. Well, Richard did. But Victoria wouldn't have it."

My brow furrowed. "That's just heartbreaking. Were Richard and Victoria close despite such a horrible tragedy?"

Mary took a sip of coffee and stared into the cup. "She told me Richard resented her for it for many years. But they worked through it, eventually." Mary chuckled. "But boy, did they bicker. Sometimes it was downright uncomfortable, wasn't it, Milly?"

Milly shrugged. "I thought it was funny how they gave each other hell. I remember one time when I stayed the night with them, Richard put a piece of tape over the remote control sensor, knowing Victoria's favorite show was coming on. After it really worked her up, he suggested she try changing out the batteries. I wanted to watch TV, so when she left the room, I removed the tape. That pissed Richard off so much, he left the house and went to his favorite bar down the road."

My eyes narrowed. "That seems an exaggerated thing to do. Was he still mad at you the next day?"

Milly picked through the blueberries for a plump, sweet one. "Nah. He acted perfectly normal and told us some corny jokes he'd learned from his buddies at the bar." Milly stood up and stretched. "I need some fresh air. Do you guys want to take the sailboat out? Maybe some fun will be a pleasant distraction."

Mary shooed us. "You two go ahead. I need to finish an order for a customer by tomorrow."

"Feel like sailing?" Milly asked me.

"Of course," I answered as I walked quickly towards the door. "I'll beat you down there."

"Yeah, right!" Milly responded with a giggle.

Mary yelled after us. "Be careful, girls."

Milly's dad always had a refrigerator packed with beer in his garage near the pier, so we packed a six-pack, some bottled waters, and some hearty snacks into a cooler then went on our way.

The sailboat we'd sailed on hundreds of times awaited us, bobbing gently in the water, with its sails fluttering in the breeze like eager wings. The sun cast a warm golden glow over the scene, and the distant calls of seagulls added life to the coastal air.

As I put one foot onto the boat, I felt the dock sway slightly beneath us, causing a familiar, soothing feeling to encompass me. Milly was right. This would be good for her.

Once we were settled in the boat, Milly took the tiller, her hands confidently guiding our course. I adjusted the sail with practiced ease, the canvas snapping taut as the wind caught it. With a gentle push, we glided away from the dock, the water beneath us rippling with every passing wave.

The boat responded to our movements, and the sensation of freedom washed over me. The gentle sway of the boat and the soft lap of water against the hull created a comforting rhythm. Each breeze played with our hair and cooled our skin.

Once we had everything set, Milly de-capped our beers. "It's Miller time, Olive," she said, handing me one.

"Cheers," we said, clanking the bottles together.

As we sailed, the world around us seemed to slow down. We chatted and laughed, sharing childhood stories and inside jokes while the salt-laden air filled our lungs. The scent of seaweed and the distant hint of a fisherman's catch filled my nose. There was nothing but sensory heaven all around us, and Milly agreed, judging by the contented smile on her face.

Time was lost to us. Minutes turned to hours, and before we knew it, the sun began its descent toward the horizon, casting a warm orange glow across the sky that was mirrored in the surrounding water.

With a reluctant sigh, we turned the boat back toward the dock.

"This was such a great time, Milly. I'm glad you thought of it. How are you feeling?"

She nodded. "Better. Yeah, we should do this more often. I really needed it."

Just then, my phone buzzed, vibrating against my side. I picked it up and glanced at the screen. "Wait, stop. Fred is calling," I stated with a hitch in my voice.

"Put him on speaker, please."

I gave her a hesitant look.

Her mouth made a straight line. "Do it, Olive. Now."

I closed my eyes for a second. "Hey, Fred. Milly is with me, and I have you on speaker."

There was a brief pause.

"Fred?"

"I'm here, kiddo. Although I don't think it's a goo—"

"Spit it out, Fred," Milly said, leaning in. "I need to know what's up."

He sighed heavily. "I've got some bad news, girls."

Milly's eyes grew wide. "But you said you didn't—"

"I know what I said, Milly. But I was wrong. Someone poisoned the chowder."

My stomach flipped inside out, making me drop my phone.

Rummaging into the hull, Milly yanked my phone back up. "That's impossible, Fred. There's no way." She vigorously shook her head. "No way."

Groaning, Fred continued. "It's true. Someone murdered Victoria Thorne. And we will find out who did it real soon. I promise you that, Milly."

She rubbed her temple. "I was the last one to handle the chowder, which makes me the prime suspect," she added, her voice breaking.

"I'm not going to lie to you. For now, it does. For now...but we'll put an end to it quickly."

With a shaky hand, Milly handed the phone back to me. She bent over the side of the boat and vomited.

"Milly," Fred calmly said, "Tell me you understand everything is going to be okay. I want to hear you say it."

"Fred, she can't right this minute."

"What is that noise? Is Milly throwing up?"

I cleared my throat. "Um. Yes. Everything we've eaten and drank today."

"Well, that wasn't the response I asked for."

"No," I agreed. "Not even close."

3

— · —

"You can't be here." Fred stopped me after Milly had walked past into the police station.

"Fred, you know I'm going to get involved either way," I responded in a firmer tone than I had ever taken with him.

"Olivia...Milly is the prime suspect." He had dropped his voice to a whisper, glancing back to make sure Milly wasn't behind him. "You know that compromises you hanging around this case. I've let you do it plenty in the past, but I have to draw the line."

I stared at him, silently. I refused to cede my ground. After a few moments, he sighed and turned.

"Come with me," he said, gruffly without even looking at me.

He led me to his office, opened the door, and waved his hand for me to come inside. After we stepped in, he shut the door.

"I get it, Olivia. I really do. But I don't know what you think I'm going to do. This isn't some game. Someone was murdered, and I have to figure out who did it. You cannot be messing around on this case." "So I'm just supposed to sit by while my best friend suffers? No way, Fred. No way." I watched his face for anger at my blatant disregard for his instructions. "You know I'm not just going to let this go."

He sighed and sat down behind his desk, putting his head in his hands. He looked up at me slowly, shaking his head.

"We're short-staffed," he grunted.

"And…" I said hesitantly. I couldn't help the slight smile that came to my face. The man knew I wasn't giving up.

"You can be a part of this but under two conditions."

"Anything," I responded, feeling a weight off my shoulders.

"First, you are an official consultant. You are under my direction. You can't go making your own decisions and doing whatever you want. Good news is that we'll pay you.""Okay," I agreed, knowing that I might just have to be a bit sneakier in some cases.

"Second, you cannot share anything with Milly." He paused as if waiting for me to argue, but I didn't. "She's a suspect. You're officially involved now. You cannot tell her a single bit of information from the case.""Okay. And that's it?"

"That's it." He sat back in his chair. "What do you think?"

"Honestly, I don't care. I'll do whatever it takes for Milly."

***

As I waited for Fred to return with the requested waters for Milly, Antonio, and Nancy, the interrogation room's atmosphere felt charged with anxiety and a heavy unspoken weight of suspicions. I couldn't help but notice Antonio and Nancy regarding Milly with what looked like confusion and shock. To think they'd already made their minds up about Milly made my blood boil. While it was true that she was the last person to handle the chowder, I would have thought they'd have more faith in someone they'd known for several years. The three had worked at the clam chowder booth for the last six years at least.

The room's temperature was frigid, a contrast to the rising emotions that simmered beneath the surface. Hard surfaces and sterile surroundings created an environment that left little room for comfort and ease, amplifying the sense of vulnerability that I imagined typically accompanied this room. This time, though, with everything feeling personal, the dilemma seemed more exaggerated.

I gave my bestie a reassuring smile, which I doubt looked convincing. Milly's eyes were wide with fright, and she looked like she wanted to curl up in the corner and cry. She'd stopped trying to talk with the other two in the room, apparently having come to the same conclusion I did. Fighting the urge to bang Nancy and Antonio's heads together, I went and sat next to Milly for support.

Fred returned with bottled water for everyone. Antonio and Nancy opened theirs, but Milly didn't even glance at it. Her hands stayed on her lap as she picked on her cuticles.

Taking out his spiral-bound notebook and a pen, Fred took a seat. "Thanks for coming. I'll make this as quick as possible," he said, glancing at each of them. "Before we begin, I'd like to introduce Olivia to you all. I know you know her, but please recognize that she is now no longer here as just a friend or acquaintance. The department has officially brought her on as a consultant to the investigation." He paused, glancing at each of them. "As you know, you are here for questioning regarding the murder of Victoria Thorne, and you are here of your own accord. That being said, I cannot divulge any details about the method used to kill the victim, so please do not ask questions about this ongoing investigation. Now, I'd like to ask Antonio and Nancy to go with the officer standing at the door. I'll bring you back in one at a time for questioning once I have questioned Milly."

Nancy sneered. "Why does Milly get to go first? Because she's your friend?"

Fred cocked his head to the side. "Because that's how this is going to go."

Antonio stood and pointed. "She is the guilty party here. Not us."

The other officer batted his hand in the air. "You two come with me. You're not under arrest now, but if you keep this up, that might change."

Fred waited until the door shut before getting up to give Milly a hug. "Everything is going to be okay. I give you my word." He tilted her chin up. "You hear me?"

She nodded.

He squeezed her shoulder before sitting back down. "Alright. Let's get started. So when and where did you cook the chowder?"

Milly rubbed her neck. "We cooked at Antonio's house. We got there at six thirty and finished up a little after eight."

"This may sound silly to ask, but how do you make clam chowder?"

"Are you planning to make it for Mrs. O'Malley this evening?" she asked, smirking.

My bestie's sense of humor made me smile, and my shoulders relaxed a bit. It seemed Fred's words of encouragement were finally sinking in.

Fred winked. "No. I plan on giving her the recipe and drinking a beer while she makes it for me."

"Somehow I don't think that's how it will work," I interjected with a chuckle.

Milly took a deep breath. "It's so easy, it's ridiculous. First, you clean and prepare the clams."

"Prepare? What does this entail?"

"Oh yeah, details. Okay, so my dad gave us the fresh clams from the day's catch. So, I knew they would be good ones, with intact shells and a nice ocean smell. Still, we didn't skip the second step which is to inspect them. You discard any clams with broken shells or ones that don't close when tapped."

"Why the ones that don't close when tapped?"

"It means the clam may be dead. Only clams that are alive when potted are safe to consume. Otherwise, it could pose a food safety risk."

Fred wrinkled his nose. "Ooh-kay, I suppose that makes sense."

"Right. Then you soak them in salt water. About a fourth cup of salt per gallon. They should soak for about thirty minutes. This expels any sand or grit. Next, you scrub the shells clean under cold running water."

Fred nodded. "Got it."

Milly proceeded to tell him the cooking instructions.

He finished jotting the last step down. "You mentioned seasonings? What did you add?"

"Antonio and Nancy added their own seasonings. I only added my miso paste. It's made of soybean puree, salt, and a fermented fungus called koji. The paste gives the chowder a unique, robust flavor. It's our secret ingredient, and it's why we win every year."

"Fermented means the paste sits around for a long time, right?"

"Yes, in this case, the koji fermented for three months."

"That's a long time."

"Not really. The length of time pumps it full of probiotics. Ever heard of kimchi? That's fermented cabbage. Kimchi ferments for much longer than three months. Actually, when consumed, fermented food offers several health benefits."

"That's...interesting. Okay, so during the cooking, how were Nancy and Antonio acting?"

Milly shrugged. "Their usual selves. Antonio takes everything way too seriously, and Nancy is just a weird bird. I'd feel bad saying as much before this happened, but since they think I'm a killer, so what? I might even ask Nancy if she's half Vulcan ... with those pointy ears of hers. And then I might ask Antonio if he plans to save Rapunzel with those nose hairs he's been neglecting."

Fred and I tried to stifle laughter, which resulted in him snorting and me choking on my wayward swallow of air.

Fred cleared his throat. "This is serious, Milly. Right now, you need to perceive me as a detective, okay?"

"Sorry, Fred," Milly replied. "I use humor when stressed. But I'll reel it in."

"Was anyone left alone with the chowder after they separated it into the smaller tasting pot?" he asked.

Milly peered up at the ceiling. "Um, I used the bathroom twice, and they were both in the kitchen went I did so. I guess one of them could have gone to use the other bathroom or whatever in my absence. Otherwise, no."

"Do you know of any animosity or grudge Antonio or Nancy might have had toward Victoria?"

"Nothing crazy. I remember one year Victoria judged an Italian dinner competition, and Nancy was a contestant. Victoria put the hammer down and harshly critiqued Nancy. She was never too keen on Victoria after that. With Antonio? No, nothing comes to mind."

"When was the Italian dinner competition?"

"It was last fall. I remember because we were investigating the White/Moore case at the time."

"Aw, yes. That was an interesting case for sure." Fred stood and stretched before straightening his uniform. "Milly, I know you were close to Victoria, and I'm very sorry for your loss. Give my condolences to your mom and dad for me." He gave her another hug. "Do me a favor, will you?"

"Yeah. Anything."

He patted her cheek. "You may have accusers. They may say nothing, but you might receive some odd looks in the coming days. But you need to keep your head up."

"Oh, the judgmental looks have already started. But I'll try to take your advice."

I stood up and put my arm around Milly. "I could not believe the way Nancy and Antonio were trying to throw you under the bus."

Fred harrumphed. "This kind of thing can bring people's true colors out. They're scared. Pointing the blame at you gets the attention off of them. Or, so they think, anyway."

Milly crossed her arms. "I know you and Olive can't discuss the investigation with me. How long do you think it will take to clear my name?"

"This really stinks to say, but I doubt we'll be able to discuss the case with you until we catch the perpetrator. I'm sorry, Milly."

Milly frowned. "But you know I'm innocent, so why not? Me and Olive have never kept secrets from one another."

"No, but you've never been a suspect in a murder investigation. Don't get involved, Milly. Doing so might make you look more suspicious."

"And," I added to let Fred know I agreed, "giving my best friend insight to an ongoing case would discredit me and my work. I'm officially helping the department now. It's different than before"

"True, kiddo," Fred agreed. "For now, I want you to take Milly home. I'll question the other two, and I'll let you know how the interviews go."

"Is there anything else I can do to help?" I asked, bound and determined to clear Milly's name.

"Where is Mr. Thorne staying?" he asked.

"At Sparrow's Nest Bed-and-Breakfast," Milly replied.

Nodding, Fred glanced back at me. "Comfortable paying him a visit, kiddo?"

I gave him thumbs up. "Does a horse neigh?"

Fred glared. "Milly, does she answer you with this annoying crap?"

"Nope, just you. And it's not crap. It would be called manure," she added, winking.

Fred pointed at the door. "Alright, both of you...out of my station."

I knew he was kidding by the gruff way he often spoke, but his request was far from a jest. It contained a stern expression of determination I'd seen only a few other times, and it was only in cases that entailed people he cared about being affected by the outcome.

Halfway to her parents' house, Milly loudly groaned. "How am I going to tell them?"

I gripped my steering wheel, turning my knuckles white. "Maybe you shouldn't. Not unless a time comes when it's absolutely necessary."

"I don't want Mom and Dad finding out from someone else. You know how this kind of stuff runs like wildfire, Olive? This would crush them more than they're already going to be."

She was right, of course. "Maybe it will be better coming from me. I can quickly reassure them that Fred is doing everything he can to clear your name. I'll explain how he won't have to waste time getting a search warrant. Once they search your house and find nothing, some of the heat will be smothered. And when the leftover miso paste tests negative for poison, you'll be off the hot seat. By then, we'll have plenty of other suspects in the hot seat."

"But me and my parents won't know when those things happen."

"No, but I will. And while I won't be able to provide details, I'll let you know the best way I can. And before long, we'll make an arrest, and all of this will be behind you."

Milly covered her mouth with a gasp. "What if someone set me up?"

My brow furrowed. "How would a setup be possible?"

Her voice sounded agitated. "It wouldn't be a setup if I knew how, now would it?"

4

— • —

NESTLED ON THE WESTSIDE of Sparrow Haven, Sparrow's Nest Bed-and-Breakfast stood as a picturesque retreat, invoking a sense of cozy warmth. A white picket fence surrounded the property as a testament to its inviting charm. Ivy vines cascaded gently along the trellises which lined the cobblestone pathway that meandered from the gate to the front steps.

The inn itself boasted a colonial-style architecture, with clapboard siding painted in a calming shade of light blue. Each window was adorned with crisp white shutters that framed the views of the rolling green landscape. Hanging flower baskets swayed in the breeze above the porch that extended along the front of the home, complete with several white rocking chairs.

The entryway of the bed-and-breakfast welcomed guests with polished hardwood floors and a braided area rug in the center. An antique front desk sat next to a white-washed, oak mantle fireplace.

After ringing the desk bell, I waited next to a bookshelf, scanning the book's spines while gathering my thoughts.

After a few moments, the owner of the establishment entered to greet me. I didn't know Edith Longmire well, but she was a frequent member of my library, so I considered her a casual friend.

She patted the back of a plush armchair. "Please have a seat, Olivia. Am I correct in assuming you are here to speak with poor Mr. Thorne? My staff and I are in complete shock."

I took a seat after she did. "Yes, thank you. I'm so sorry for your loss. I know Victoria stayed here anytime she visited our village."

"Yes, she did." Edith dabbed at her misty eyes. "Richard usually returns from supper around seven. Would you like to wait in the kitchen? I was just about to put some tea on."

Glancing at my phone, I nodded. The time was fifteen 'til, and I could use a cup of tea after an emotional day with Milly and her parents. No matter how much reassurance I tried to offer them, they were still sick with worry for their daughter, on top of mourning a close friend who should still be alive.

"That sounds good. Thank you," I said, following her to the kitchen.

The dining area of the house exuded the same sense of intimacy and rustic elegance as the parlor. Edith pulled out the head chair at a long communal table below a wrought-iron chandelier. The table was set with fine China and crystal glassware. I took a deep breath in, enjoying the three spiced-vanilla candles burning on the countertop.

"How has business been so far this summer, Edith?"

She filled a brass kettle with water. "Oh, it's been a record breaker. The summer fair and other new community events have boosted our numbers tremendously."

"That's wonderful. How many employees do you have currently?"

Edith set the kettle on the gas stove before spinning the front left dial to high. "I employ two chefs and two housekeepers. With just the four rooms, the five of us manage well enough and allow for ample time off. I believe in a balanced work-personal life."

Being careful to listen for the front door, I asked my next question casually. "I'm sure your employees appreciate your thoughtfulness. What's it like to have couples from different walks of life stay in your home?"

She laughed. "It's all over the board. Sometimes we learn more about our patrons than we'd like to."

Nodding, I smiled. "Oh, I can imagine. I was wondering...how did Victoria and Richard get along during their stays here over the years?"

Edith put a chamomile tea bag in each cup while making a tsk sound. "They were entertaining, to say the least, constantly teasing one another during breakfast."

"Sounds like a fun, youthful-type marriage," I said, prompting a response.

"Well, teasing might be the wrong word," she said, pouring hot water into two ceramic mugs. "Cream, sweetener, or both, Olivia?"

"Plain is fine. Thank you."

Edith set the steaming mugs down and took the nearest seat. "Victoria and Richard lost a child. Most marriages don't make it after such a horrific loss. I've always admired the fact that they pulled through."

"Would you say they had a happy marriage, then?"

She took a sip of tea before replying in a soft tone. "Listen, Olivia, I know you have a job to do. But I will not infringe upon their private lives by sharing opinions derived from their staying here. I hope you understand."

"Of course. I understand. And I respect your position." I glanced down at my cup. "This tea is excellent. Thank you," I added right before hearing the front door open and then shut.

Edith smiled with a wink. "I'll give you two the room." She stood and quickly poured another mug of tea. "Richard might want something stronger, just in case. Anyway, I'll tell him you're here. I've always appreciated your dedication to our town. Good night and good luck, Olivia."

"Thank you. Your kind words mean a lot."

Edith had been correct. Richard went straight to the bar and poured some bourbon on a round-shaped ice cube he'd collected from a freezer on the shelf.

He stood at an average height with a lean build, reflecting an essence of healthy habits and moderation. Richard wore a gray sport jacket, a shade darker than his hair, and walrus mustache. As he turned towards me, I noted that his faded-brown eyes held a kindness underlined by weariness. Gray circles of puffy skin ballooned beneath them. Plopping down in the same chair Edith had sat in, he took a prolonged sip and made a contented sigh after swallowing.

The smile he gave me looked forced. "You must be the Olivia girl I've heard so much about over the years. Milly thinks of you as a sister. But I'm sure you're not here to speak about relations. I realize a left-behind spouse of a murdered one is always a suspect."

Taking the hint of forgoing formalities, I nodded. "I want you to know how very sorry I am for your loss, Mr. Thorne. Sadly, yes, anyone closest to the victim is usually the initial suspect. Seems backward, but that's the world we live in."

His mouth slightly turned up at the corners. "I see why Milly and her parents admire you. You're brutally honest yet gracefully collected. You can call me Richard, by the way. I'm not as old-fashioned as I look."

I took a sip of tea, trying to add a sense of calm to this otherwise intense conversation about to take place. "Got it. So when did you and your wife arrive in Sparrow Haven, Richard?"

He jiggled the melting ice in his glass. "Friday. We weren't sure how many days we'd stay, but we figured three or four. Outside of her tasting event schedule, Victoria and I tended to be the spontaneous sort."

"I am too. Did you always attend the events with your wife?"

"Not unless the event was on the coast. I love deep-sea fishing. So, I'd say about half the time I'd tag along. Fishing is my life. I used to be a competitive pro-fisherman."

"Wow, sounds like a fun job."

"Yeah, like they say...I've never worked a day in my life." Richard stretched, rolling his head in a full circle before looking directly into my eyes. "I loved my wife, Olivia. And someone murdered her. Someone took her from me. I kissed my wife goodbye that morning and said I'd see her at dinnertime. Turns out I didn't eat a bite, and I went to bed alone. I can't sleep and wondering who killed her is driving me mad. Yet, nobody has told me much of anything, like what the monster used to poison Victoria."

I bit my lower lip. "I'm sorry. The lab is still conducting tests. For now, all we know is that someone tampered with the chowder. That's all I can tell you."

He briefly closed his eyes. "I'm sorry. I just want answers, and I want swift justice, so I can begin to mourn her properly."

"I understand. We want the same thing. For now, I need to ask you a few questions if you're up to it. Otherwise, you could wait, and a detective will come by in the morning. Either option is totally fine. I'm sure you're exhausted."

Richard downed the rest of his glass. "I am, but now is fine."

"Alright." I took out my paper pad and pen. "Did you and Victoria have a fight before or after coming to town?"

He grunted. "We squabbled now and then, but we never out-and-out fought. At some point in a marriage, you stop the cat and dog fights, realizing nobody ever wins."

"What did you recently squabble about?"

Richard pinched the bridge of his nose. "I don't know. Petty stuff. Maybe I didn't close the refrigerator before her five second rule, or maybe she didn't pack the right deck shoes I'd requested."

"Okay, I understand. Can you tell me all the places you went to and what you did after arriving here on Friday?"

He did so and then sighed heavily. "I visited with Milly twice during that period, and I know she was a person associated with the chowder that..." He stared into space for a second before coming back to the conversation. "But I never laid eyes on any of the...ingredients. I regret that sweet Milly is a suspect more than being one myself. This must be difficult for you, too, Olivia. You're both so close."

"Yes, it is. But I'm determined to find the perpetrator...for you and for Milly and for her parents."

"I appreciate your optimism." He yawned. "I've heard of your excellent track record, so I find some comfort in knowing you're part of the investigation."

"Thank you, Richard. Do you know of anyone in town who had a grudge against Victoria?"

"Sure. Anyone she'd negatively judged in the past. You'd think as a tasting judge, my wife would know the difference between constructive criticism and insulting a chef. Victoria didn't. Doing so publicly made many of them strongly dislike her."

"Can you recall any of these chefs' names?"

"I could give you some nicknames she'd given to several of them, but that's it."

"Will you give me examples?"

He chuckled. "Let's see...there was. Flavor-floosy. Beef-jerky. Ladle-head. I won't say the more colorful ones."

I had to bite the inside of my cheeks not to laugh. "She used these nicknames only when talking to you? Or to their faces as well?"

"I'm sure it was just to me. Victoria could be mean, but I don't think she'd act that unprofessional." He yawned. "Sorry, but I need to hit the hay. Let me give you my number. Feel free to call me with any more questions or with any new information anytime of the day or night." He reached for my pen and wrote his number on the top of my open pad.

"Thanks for your time. I absolutely will." I closed my notebook and stood.

"Would it be too forward for me to ask why a nice, pretty gal like you isn't married?"

My mouth came close to dropping. He hadn't asked the question in a flirty tone, but a man who'd just lost his wife wondering this about a stranger confused me.

He spoke before I knew how to respond. "Let me guess, you've been close before but then got cold feet?"

My laugh sounded forced. "Um, I...Milly would say I have a permanent case of cold feet. But my condition may be changing. I'm dating a really great guy." I was rambling out of nerves, so I shut my mouth and headed toward the door.

But then I spun around, suddenly curious how he'd answer this next question. "Would you recommend marriage?"

Richard crossed his arms, his face suddenly stern. "You just questioned me about the murder of my wife. How do you think I'd answer your question, Olivia?"

I didn't like his answer at all. "Well, I would hope truthfully."

His tone sounded curt. "The answer is complex, and I'm whipped. Good night."

5

— • —

As I walked across the threshold of my home, an Italian aroma wafted to my nose. I heard someone in my kitchen rummaging around as Barkley came to greet me with kisses. Doubting the person would be Milly, I concluded Ethan had come over to make me dinner. I found the gesture sweet.

"I figured you'd be exhausted, so I made you parmesan chicken and a salad with extra halved cherry tomatoes the way you like it." He took our plates to the table and pulled out a chair for me with a smile.

Ethan grazed his thumb across my cheek and trailed the touch down to my chin before lightly kissing me. He took my hand and brought me to the dining table.

My stomach growled. Luckily it was quiet. "Goodness, everything looks and smells delicious, Ethan. I didn't realize how hungry I was."

He poured some wine for us. "Don't wait on me. Dig in and tell me what you think."

My teeth sunk into the crispy breaded layer then deeper into the meaty, juicy middle.

Closing my eyes, I nodded. "You outdid yourself this time. The chicken is rich and succulent. Did you make the marinara?"

He chuckled, taking a seat. "No. I used Prego and added some seasonings. I'm glad you like it." He took a sip of wine.

I stabbed a cucumber with my fork. "How was your day?"

He shrugged. "Okay, except I've been worried about you."

I reached over and squeezed his hand. "That's sweet. I just need to get focused on solving this crime and stop dwelling on the personal side of things. If Fred catches a glimpse of my anxiety, he'll take me off this case faster than Barkley runs after a squirrel." I sipped my wine. "What did you do all day? Besides playing gourmet chef?"

"I took my boat for a sail with Norman. You know, the guy I met at the gym?"

"Oh nice! Milly and I went sailing...when was it? Yesterday? My days are running together."

His eyes lit up. "Hey, we should set Milly up with Norman. He's seven years older, but the dude's nice looking, in great shape, and he seems to be a good guy. He's funny and makes decent money, too."

I winked. "Are you sure you don't want to date him?"

He laughed. "I'm just saying, Norman checks all the boxes of what Milly wants in a man."

My brow lifted. "True. But what if they don't work out, and then the breakup makes things weird between you two?"

He pointed his fork at me. "I'd be worried about that, truly—if I weren't a guy. Men don't care about stuff like that."

I playfully rolled my eyes. "Of course. What was I thinking?"

He cleared his throat. "May I say something about the case or would you rather—"

"Of course, you can, Ethan. You're my assistant, and a decent one at that," I added kiddingly. He'd been a darn dutiful assistant in the last two cases.

"What I have to say isn't directly related to the case itself. It's about Fred."

"Oh, okay." I popped a cherry tomato in my mouth.

"I think Fred is keeping important information from you."

My brow lifted. "Why do you think that?"

"One of his detectives came to the clinic. His puppy needed shots. Anyway, the detective said they know what poison the perpetrator used, so leads should start emerging."

I sharply inhaled, choking on my unchewed bite. Taking a swig of wine, the food finally went down.

"You okay?"

I clutched my throat. "Yeah." I coughed again before draining my glass. "I don't understand. Fred asked me to question Victoria's husband. So why would he withhold the type of poison from me?"

Ethan shrugged. "Maybe Fred is giving you just enough work to keep you happy, but he's limiting your involvement because of Milly. He may think you're too close to this to be objective." He threw his hands in the air. "I could be wrong, though."

"You could be right. When did the detective visit your clinic?"

"The day after the fatal tasting. He was my last appointment, so about six-thirty."

I hit the table with my fist. "Fred knew the poison the killer used when he called to inform me of the murder."

"Was Milly with you?"

"Yes, but he could have told me a hundred times since then."

"Honey, at least Fred is still allowing you to be involved in some capacity."

"Don't 'honey' me. How can I solve the crime if I don't have the needed information?"

He cocked a brow. "First of all, I will 'honey' you all I want. Second, I agree. You need to talk to him. But in person, so you can show him the effective puppy dog look."

Refilling my glass, I huffed. "I'm so mad. I'm not sure the puppy look is possible."

"No, you got this. If you want to win, muster it up...*honey*."

I smirked. "You're right, *honey*."

"I should have recorded you saying so," he said with a wink.

"Well? What's the name of the poison?"

"Hemlock."

I reached for my phone.

"I've already done a bit of research."

Setting my phone back down, I leaned in. "I'm all ears."

"And cute ears too. Anyway, the poison is called hemlock, aka, conium maculatum. Hemlock contains alkaloids, which affect the nervous system and can lead to paralysis and respiratory failure. Ingesting even a small amount of hemlock can be fatal."

"Is it a plant?"

"It's a wild biennial herbaceous belonging to the carrot family. The seeds and the roots are the most toxic part, but all the parts are poisonous."

"Where does this plant grow?"

"Here. Hemlock grows in every state except Alaska, Florida, Hawaii, and Mississippi."

Just then, my phone buzzed.

I cackled. "Uh-huh. Speak of the devil...Hey, Fred."

"Hey, kiddo. I've got some good news."

"Finally. Let me have it," I said, sighing.

"The miso paste is clean. The lab ran the test a few times to be sure."

"So, no trace of hemlock?"

Silence.

"Surely, you didn't think I wouldn't find out, Fred."

He grunted. "No, not for a while, anyway, because we're not releasing the information to the public. How did you find out?"

"Seriously, Fred. How could you withhold this from me?"

"I have my reasons. For one, you're too close to this, kiddo."

"You're close to Milly too. Why did you let me question Richard Thorne, then?"

"Because I was avoiding this conversation. Now, answer my question."

"One of your detective's pets is Ethan's patient."

"Was it Detective Schulz?"

Ethan could apparently hear Fred. He nodded.

"Yes. Is he in trouble?" I asked sarcastically.

"He didn't follow orders. I had my reasons, kiddo."

"I'm hurt, Fred. This investigation means everything to me. I already promised to keep...wait, what does this mean for Milly?"

"She's not off the list. But since Milly made the paste, and it's clean, this bodes well for her."

"Okay. But she's still a prime suspect..."

"Yes, but Nancy and Antonio didn't have access to the miso. If the miso paste had come back positive for hemlock, Milly would have been arrested. Obviously, all three of them had access to the chowder. Untainted miso should take some of the limelight off of her."

I rubbed my throbbing temple. "I guess so. Now, she's just sharing the limelight with two other suspects. To be honest, this doesn't make me feel any better, Fred."

"I know, but I was relieved. I was scared to death the miso would come back positive for hemlock."

"Fred, you put me on this case."

"I know. And I'm sorry for withholding the hemlock. I feel like a turd now, kiddo."

"You should," I said teasingly.

"Tell me how the questioning went with Richard."

So, I did, including the talk with Edith beforehand, and the end when the conversation with Richard got a little weird.

"Sounds like the interview went well. Gives me some things to think about, especially knowing Victoria was in the habit of insulting local chefs. Alright, breakfast tomorrow, kiddo?"

"See you there," I answered.

Hitting end, I caught Ethan looking at me oddly.

"What? Do I have something on my face?"

"A cute, little nose. No, I'm curious about the last part of the questioning."

Because Ethan was listening, I didn't tell Fred what I'd said about having a permanent cold feet condition, or how it was changing.

"About asking Richard if he would recommend marriage?" I asked, feeling my face burn.

"That's the one," he replied, reaching for the wine bottle.

I shrugged. "I was just curious to know his answer. And I was glad because of how he responded. It sounded to me like he might not have recommended marriage if it weren't for him being a suspect in his wife's murder investigation. Don't you?"

He swirled the wine in his glass. "He said the answer was complex. You said he and his wife lost a child, right? A loss so deep would make any marriage difficult. Maybe that's what he meant."

"Could be. Milly's mom told me Richard resented Victoria for not wanting any more children. This fact could be a motive. I hope not. Milly and her parents are close to him."

He set his glass down. "I think you left out part of the conversation because I'm here. Why did marriage come up?"

The skin on my arm prickled. "Because his wife died," I said, a bit defensively.

Ethan grunted. "Fine. If you don't want to tell me." He waved dismissively. "Suit yourself."

I rolled my eyes. "I really don't need a guilt trip right now, Ethan."

"If you feel guilty, that's on you. I simply said you don't have to tell me."

I wanted to lie and say there wasn't anything else to tell, but Ethan knew me too well. And I wasn't in the habit of lying. So, I smiled and got up to clean the kitchen.

Ethan did likewise, but he had little to say for the rest of the night.

6

—.—

THE NEXT MORNING, FRED said he'd pick up some breakfast for us from Vivi's café and meet me at a bookstore owned by a mutual friend of ours.

As I walked in, the bell above the door jingled softly, announcing my presence to the cozy world within. The warm sunlight filtered through the windows, casting a soft glow on the worn wooden floors. The air carried a faint scent of old paper, ink, and a subtle aroma of freshly brewed coffee.

My eyes wandered across the shelves stretching from floor to ceiling, showcasing a treasure trove of literary gems waiting to be explored. I could hear the soft rustling of pages being turned by patrons and a low chatter buzzed the vicinity.

Martin Lewis, the owner of Turn the Page, waved at me before holding a finger up for me to wait while he assisted a patron. Martin was a quiet, unassuming man who loved sharing his vast knowledge of books and literature with others. His light-brown hair, graying at the temples, was tousled from time spent perusing the shelves with his patrons. Tall, with a slender build and a pair of round glasses perched on his nose, Martin had an air of quiet intelligence people found both comforting and intriguing.

I'd spent countless hours in this bookstore, doing casework over the years, and Martin assisted me in my research whenever time and business allowed.

Taking a seat in my usual spot, I flipped through my notes until Martin approached me with a hug.

He said his usual greeting. "If it isn't my favorite sleuth of Sparrow Haven."

I smiled. "It's good to see you, Martin. Business seems to be good."

He glanced around the vicinity. "Patrons come and go in waves. This shop is either popping like popcorn or dead as a doornail."

I nodded. "The library is the same way some days."

"Did you take the day off?" he asked, scooting his glasses up higher on his button nose.

"Actually, Milly and I took the week off. We planned to spend some time at the fair and get into trouble along the way. I suppose we got more than we bargained for."

"I'll say...How's sweet Milly holding up?"

"As well as you could expect. She's staying with her parents this week."

Annoyed with a curl dangling in my eyes, I yanked a band I had put on my wrist and gathered my hair into a ponytail.

Martin shook his head. "I bet it's difficult not having her help on this investigation. Not to mention the stress of it all. I'm so sorry, Olivia."

"It is difficult, but I'll manage."

He motioned for me to follow. "How about a cup of coffee?"

A moment later, Fred walked in and waved, heading toward us in the coffee area.

Martin poured three cups of coffee, and then we went to sit at one of the pub-styled tables.

"Here's your boring fruit and yogurt bowl, kiddo," Fred said, pulling it from the bag.

He handed Martin a BLT and then pulled an enormous apple fritter out for himself. "Vivi's café is to blame for my fat gut. If she didn't make these, I wouldn't be able to eat them."

I laughed. "You'd just find someone else to buy from to indulge that sweet tooth of yours."

He patted his midsection. "True, but then it would be their fault, too."

"How are you and the wife doing, Fred?" Martin asked.

"Well, Mrs. O'Malley hasn't killed me in my sleep, so good as gold. What about you?"

"Same. Just don't tell my Annie about hemlock."

Clearing his throat, Fred shifted uncomfortably in his chair as I sent him a glare.

Martin glanced from me to Fred. "Is something wrong?"

I picked up a strawberry and popped the plump berry in my mouth. "Fred wasn't going to tell me what the killer used to poison Mrs. Thorne."

Martin chuckled. "In the doghouse, are you, Fred?"

"You could say that," he said between chews.

"How is Olivia supposed to solve this crime without knowing—"

Fred raised a hand. "I know. Believe me. I'll probably never hear the end of this."

Martin nodded. "You withheld the type of poison because of Milly, right?" He batted at the air. "Olivia is capable of separating the two and remaining objective."

"Well, if I see otherwise, she's off the case."

I huffed. "Hello? Will you guys stop talking as if I'm not here?"

Martin stood. "Oh boy, sorry, Olivia." He glanced across the store. "The next wave just arrived. I'll check back soon."

Fred rubbed his eyes. "Alright. You can call me a turd one time, and then this quarrel is over. Not another word about it, kiddo."

"Elephant-turd."

"Ha-ha. Cute. Okay," he said, yanking his pad out. "Let's discuss the questioning I conducted with Nancy and Antonio."

Nodding, I took a sip of coffee.

"As it happens, Antonio is the jealous type. The way he talks, I can tell he's threatened by any chef who is more successful than him. As far as Victoria, Antonio held her in high regard. He proudly mentioned how they enjoyed talking smack about local chefs. He said Victoria made it clear who her favorites were, as well as who she considered amateurs. Regarding Milly, he claims she acted nervous and fidgety the morning of the tasting."

"They were getting ready for a competition, so what?" I asked defensively.

"Don't."

I slapped my leg. "What?"

"You don't need to defend Milly. You and I know she isn't the killer, but we have a responsibility to hear everyone out. In this casework, Milly is a suspect for now. That's the cold, hard truth."

I bit my lower lip. "I know, Fred."

Fred tapped his pen on the table. "I think you know it, but you have to accept it. Repeat after me. Milly is a suspect."

I shook my head. "Stop being ridiculous."

He leaned in and spoke slowly. "Say it, Olivia Harper, or so help me—"

"Milly is a suspect. There. Happy?"

"No, not at all. But this is our current reality. And our duty is to prove she shouldn't be a suspect and get her name erased from the list."

"I'm sorry. You're right. What part did Antonio play in making the chowder?"

Fred flipped to the next page. "That's more like it. Good question. Antonio provided the vegetables for the chowder. He collected them from his personal garden. They decided on adding carrots, mushrooms, and artichokes. Antonio roasted the veggies to create caramelization before adding them to the broth. When I asked him if he knew what hemlock was. He said yes and that he knew the plant was poisonous."

"Why would Antonio know about hemlock?"

"He claims only the best culinary experts who grow their own produce make it their business to know such things. For example, Antonio rattled off the name of every poisonous mushroom that grows in this area. And then he listed the ones safe to consume."

"So, once they finished making the chowder, who poured a portion of it into the tasting pot?"

"Antonio did. He says Milly and Nancy were right there with him, cleaning."

"If Antonio's back was to them, he could have added the crushed hemlock seeds without them noticing. Especially if the ladies were busy cleaning the kitchen."

Fred nodded. "Oh, no doubt. But so far, Antonio lacks real motive."

"Or the man's story is full of lies."

"It lined up fairly closely with what Nancy had to say about him. She confirmed Antonio respected Victoria to the point of openly kissing her butt. Nancy says everybody teased him about having a crush on her."

"And he's the jealous type? How big of a crush? I'd say there's your motive."

Fred titled his head. "Yeah, maybe. If he couldn't have her, then…"

"If it's okay, I'll look into this lead?"

"Sure, you thought of it."

"What else did you uncover with Nancy?"

"She's an ambitious chef. Milly was right. Victoria harshly and publicly critiqued Nancy last fall at an Italian tasting."

"I'm surprised she told you."

"Nancy didn't admit it. I asked Antonio about Victoria and Nancy's relationship. The harsh critiquing was the first thing out of his mouth. When I asked Nancy about the tasting, she downplayed the occasion. She said she's gotten used to being critiqued and has developed a thick skin. She knew Victoria was just doing her job, so it didn't affect their relationship in the slightest."

"But Milly said Nancy wasn't too keen on Victoria after the Italian tasting, remember?"

"I do."

"I'll try to find out more details about Victoria and Nancy's relationship."

"Alright. And one more thing…the station received an anonymous letter. The person wanted to make us aware of a feud between Victoria and a guy named Ben Fields. He's a former restaurateur who had a publicized dispute with Victoria a few months back."

"What was the dispute about?"

"The letter didn't say anything else." Fred paused, tapping his chin. "Did you ask Milly if they ever left the tasting pot unattended?"

I scratched my head. "No. I guess I've been too focused on whether Nancy or Antonio were ever alone with it. Duh. Why didn't I think of asking such an obvious question?"

Fred stood and stretched. "I could tell you were in too much shock at first to think clearly. This is why I was reluctant to tell you about the poison. Now that you've had time to wrap your head around it, I can tell all four cylinders are back up and running," he added with a wink.

"Ooh. Now, I understand. I'm sorry for giving you grief, Fred. You had every right to make sure my head would clear up."

"It's okay, kiddo. It was still a turd thing to do. We all had some shock to work through."

"So, what did Antonio and Nancy say when you asked them?"

"They both said there was about a fifteen-minute window. Milly brought the tasting pot to the stall, and then all three of them made rounds to shake all the competitors' hands."

I nodded. "Interesting."

"That it is. So, ask Milly just to be sure she says the same thing."

"Of course. And I'll have her write a list of all the competitor's names and anyone else she can recall who was present before the tasting started."

Fred smiled. "That's my girl."

7

— • —

Milly had called me after I had left the bookstore, saying she needed an escape. She asked if I would go on a hot-air balloon ride with her in the morning, but severe weather cancelled those plans. Instead, we watched Netflix all day while binge eating our stress away.

Today, however, the weather was perfect with clouds spotting the blue sky like stepping stones, a cool breeze off of the harbor cooling my skin.

As Milly and I climbed into the woven basket of the hot-air balloon, a thrilling rush of delight filled the surrounding air. Monica, the aeronaut piloting the craft, ignited the burner, and a powerful whoosh started our ascent. The balloon responded to the controlled release of hot air, and with a gentle tug, we began our journey skyward, leaving the world with all its drama below to shrink into a mesmerizing mosaic.

The view unfolding before us was nothing short of breathtaking. Rolling landscapes sprawled in every direction, a canvas painted in lush shades of green and gold, basking in the warm embrace of the sun. The clouds glistened off the rugged edges of the distant cliffs, casting fleeting shadows over the terrain.

Amid the peaceful ambiance, the wind carried with it the earthy aroma of forests, and the invigorating tang of the sea-salted air. As

Monica navigated the skies, we found ourselves amidst the current of a flock of pelicans soaring with grace in circles around us.

As the balloon continued its ascent, sounds of civilization grew distant, replaced by a serene stillness, allowing us to absorb the beauty of our beloved New England home.

We floated in contented silence for several minutes, allowing the stress and anxiety to subside, as if being carried layer-by-layer with every gust of wind.

Running my fingers across the basket's woven texture, I nudged Milly, and we smiled at one another.

"I never want to go back down," Milly said. "Not until all this craziness is over."

I draped my arm around her shoulders. "Fred and I are beginning to make some headway into our investigation. I promise this nightmare will be over soon, Milly."

Out of the corner of my eyes, I saw the pilot's head turn toward us, her eyes growing wide, but she remained silent. I had hoped Milly wouldn't notice, but she did. With a roll of her eyes, Milly shook her head, turning to face the woman, who looked about our age, with bright red hair and hazel eyes.

I held my breath, shaking my head at Milly. Judging by the intense expression on her face, something outlandish was about to come out of her mouth.

And out the words came. "Don't worry, you're not hundreds of feet up in the air with a murderer."

The woman sent her a skeptical expression.

I nudged Milly, but she wouldn't back down. "You got something to say to me?" she asked, crossing her arms.

I could hardly believe my ears when Monica broke out in boisterous laughter. She stopped, only to catch her breath. "Sorry, I just..." She burst out into laughter again.

"Just what?" Milly asked, looking as confused as I felt. "Spit it out already. What's so funny?"

She smiled from ear to ear. "I wouldn't give a rat's ass if you did kill the old hag."

Milly's eyes narrowed. "What? Did you know Victoria Thorne?"

Monica nodded. "Yep. It's a small world after all. Am I right?"

"How did you come to know her?" I asked.

"Victoria put my mother's restaurant out of business."

"When? How?" Milly asked in a high-pitched tone.

She glanced out of the corner of her eye. "Um, about ten years ago. After her last visit to my mom's tavern, Victoria wrote bad reviews all over the internet. She lied, saying she'd gotten food poisoning and almost died from eating at the tavern, and the story made the local newspaper."

"What was the name of your mom's business?" I asked.

"I doubt you've heard of it. Her restaurant wasn't in this town. It was located in Ballentine. But whatever...she named the place The Hillside Tavern. The place went from booming to closed in a matter of weeks. My mom should have waited it out longer, but she was too embarrassed and threw in the towel."

I shook my head. "How terrible. I'm so sorry for...what's your mother's name?" I asked, as casually as I could muster.

Cursing, Monica's hand flew to her head. "Um. Can you two just enjoy the flight? I need to focus on our descent."

Milly huffed. "You know, we can easily find out what her name is."

"I'd rather you not involve my mom. Like I said, all this happened a long time ago. Just please forget this entire conversation."

"You know I can't do that," I gently stated.

Tears pooled in her eyes. "My mother is sick...cancer. If you have a heart, you'll drop this."

I frowned. "How terrible. I'm very sorry. What kind of cancer?"

"Lung cancer. Stage two. The baffling thing is, she's never smoked a single cigarette in her life."

I shook my head. "Gosh. We certainly wish her the best, Monica. Truly."

As the hot-air balloon began descending, the once vast expanse above and below started to narrow, and the ground drew closer with each breath.

The tranquil beauty around us starkly contrasted with the palpable tension lingering in the air between us and Monica. The gentle hum of the burner was the only sound breaking the awkward silence as we glided toward the tree line.

Bound and determined not to allow the exchange to dampen our excursion, I turned to face the view. The breeze, once crisp and invigorating at higher altitudes, now bore a softened warmth on my face as the world gradually took on more defined shapes.

As Monica's hands made skillful maneuvers with apparent ease, I was ready to be free of the tension hovering unspoken in the basket.

I felt bad for Monica. Whether or not she knew it, her sick mother was now part of a murder investigation. The conversation we'd just had left me without an option.

I was also relieved Milly let the subject drop, but her former restlessness had returned, judging by the way she fidgeted with her fingernails. So much for our needed escape. Still, I'd gained a lead, making this trip worth every minute.

We said our uncomfortable goodbyes, and once we'd gotten a way away from the balloon site, Milly broke into a run toward my car.

***

"You need to eat, Milly," I said, pointing at the untouched chicken wrap on the coffee table.

She clapped her hands. "I will, but this calls for a celebration." Milly got up and returned with a champagne bottle and two glasses.

"What are you talking about? Celebrate what?"

She poured the drinks before answering. "We have the name of the killer. I found Monica's mom, Cathy Simons. She's the one whodunit, Olive. I can feel it in my bones."

Reaching for the offered glass, I shook my head. "What you are feeling is unrealistic expectations."

Milly went to clang our glasses in cheer, but I pulled mine away.

"What the heck?" she asked, glaring.

I set my glass down and gripped her shoulders. "Listen to me, Milly. You're not thinking rationally. I know you want the killer found, like yesterday. But you're drawing a ridiculous conclusion without any proof. This isn't like you."

She held her hand up. "Hear me out. She had motive, clear as day. And the woman has a death sentence hanging over her head. So, if she's caught, so what?"

I groaned. "You know what? I'm done talking about this. Period."

"But Olive—"

I raised my voice. "I will look into Cathy. And yes, she's a suspect, but you and I are not going to discuss this any further."

"But—"

I stood up. "But nothing. I'm sorry, but you know what Fred said."

Milly slumped down on the couch. "Fine."

I took a seat beside her. "Since we couldn't even have one day off from this case, I might as well follow up with you on a few things."

"Can we talk about it over a mule?" she asked, taking the bottle and glasses back.

I glanced at my phone. "It's three o'clock."

"Well, it's five o'clock somewhere. Besides, we only have today and tomorrow left on this glorious vacation of ours."

I squeezed her hand. "You're right."

While I went to get my case folder, Milly went to the bar and made our drinks. I knew she'd pour them strong, so I intended to sip lightly, not wanting to slip up and say something I shouldn't about the investigation.

As I joined Milly, she handed me a copper mug while holding hers up. "You better not leave me hanging again," she said, laughing.

"Cheers," we said, clanging our mugs together.

I took a whiff of the cup. Yep, Milly would be in bed early this evening if she kept this up.

She lightly slapped my shoulder. "Don't judge. I'm drowning my sorrows away."

"No judgement, here." I opened my notebook. "And you, no peeking."

She stuck her tongue out.

"Okay. So, once you all arrived at the fair, what did you do?"

"We set up the chowder stall and then went to show good sportsmanship."

"Meaning?"

"We went to shake everyone's hands, wishing them luck like we always do."

"All three of you went together?"

Her eyes grew wide. "We did. So, the chowder was unattended for, I'd say...ten or fifteen minutes."

I tore a page from my notebook and slid it over to her. "Make a list of everyone you saw. Think hard. Not just competitors but anyone."

She took the offered pen. "There weren't a ton of people around before the tasting, but there were several, and I don't know all their names."

"I thought you knew everyone," I said, hoping to keep things light. Milly's brain didn't work well under stress. It didn't seem like she had even heard me.

A few moments later, she handed the paper and pen back. "If I think of anyone else, I'll let you know."

I glanced at the lengthy list. "Did you see anyone buzzing around your chowder stall while you were out talking to people?"

"I didn't pay attention. On our way back, I saw a few people, but nobody I could name. Besides, the stall has a back door, and it was open at the time. The killer likely used the back to get in. And if they ducked down, nobody would have seen them inside."

"Were you with Nancy and Antonio the whole time while making rounds?"

She took a gulp from her cup. "No, we split up for a bit, but then we walked back to the stall together. One of them could have totally gone back to it, poisoned the chowder, then returned to shake more hands."

I nodded as I jotted. "Okay. So, before...you told me Nancy didn't like Victoria."

"Right, because of the Italian tasting. Victoria ripped Nancy a new one."

"Sounds like Victoria had a mean streak."

Milly chuckled. "Yeah, but most people thought she was funny. I think harsh remarks were her way of making the tasting more entertaining and make the crowd laugh."

"Well, Nancy didn't think the cutthroat critique was funny."

"That's because my butt has more of a sense of humor than Nancy does."

I pinched my nose. "Don't prove it, please."

Milly threw her head back and laughed.

"Did Nancy ever openly make her grudge toward Victoria obvious?"

Milly rolled her eyes. "Not to Victoria's face. But Nancy gossiped to no end behind Victoria's back. Ask Nancy's coworkers. I would bet my left hand they'll say the same."

"Alright. So, next, describe Antonio's relationship with Victoria."

She snorted. "Antonio worshipped the ground she walked on."

"Is Antonio married?"

"Yes, but I don't think he's happily married. He treats his wife like crap in front of whoever is around. I don't know why Nina puts up with it."

"Did Nina know her husband adored Victoria?"

She squinted. "I don't know. Possibly."

I tapped my pen against my chin, thinking I'd pay Nina a visit tomorrow. "One more question, and then I'm downing this mule."

Milly made herself a second one. I noted that she went lighter on the booze this time. Maybe it'd be a late night after all.

"Go ahead. I'm listening, Ms. Detective."

"Do you know a Ben Fields?"

Milly rolled her eyes. "He's a client of mine, and a difficult one. The man is always trying to cut a deal. The last time Mr. Fields came in, I had to tell him my emporium wasn't a flea market."

"Did Mr. Fields know Victoria?"

She shrugged. "Maybe. He used to own a restaurant."

"Did the place close?"

"No, it's the Bistro on the Boulevard...you know, the one we like. Mr. Fields sold the place. Rumor has it he got a divorce, but he's never said so himself."

Finishing the last note, I slammed the notebook and picked up my mule.

"Now can we celebrate?" Milly asked, winking.

I sighed. "Celebrate what, silly?"

"You, Olive. I can tell you're kicking ass on this case, and I'm feeling a lot better about not going to prison for life."

I laughed. "Good. Because I'd never let that happen." I took a big swig. "Milly, would you be open to Ethan setting you up with a friend of his?"

"Shoot, if he's anything like Ethan, tell his friend to meet me down the aisle. I'll be the one in a white dress."

"Ha. Touché."

8

— . —

I NEVER CONDUCTED INTERVIEWS with suspects or otherwise over the phone. Body language and facial expressions always spoke volumes about their tone and their answers. So I knew I needed to drive to Ballentine to interview Cathy Simons.

I had told Ethan I'd wait until his clinic closed, so we could visit Ballentine together.

In the meantime, I planned to question Ben Fields to find out why an anonymous letter was sent to the station reporting a feud between him and Victoria. Fred's forensic team found a partial print on the letter's envelope—enough to uncover the sender. Linda Mills from Sparrow Haven had typed the letter. Fred planned to pay her an unexpected visit himself today.

Upon arriving at Ben Field's residence, I got out of my car and approached the mid-sized Victorian home. The white-painted exterior stood as a graceful tribute to a bygone era, adorned with ornate trimming and gingerbread detailing that evoked a sense of whimsy.

The parting clouds allowed the morning rays to gleam across the wraparound porch, where I spotted a man watering the hanging flower baskets between rockers and a quaint side table.

The man wore earbuds, so he didn't hear me approaching. I didn't want to start an interview by startling the man half to death, so I stood grounded and pondered on how to get his attention. Wave my arms in the air, perhaps?

Luckily, a woman with silver hair gathered in a tight bun opened the door and waved me to come up. She began tapping the man on his shoulder. He jumped back, raising a fist up in a defensive manner. The women lightly shoved him before pointing in my direction. I took the first of six steps and put a pleasant expression on my face.

The man's mouth dropped open, but he quickly shut it back while yanking the earbuds out.

I extended my hand to the woman and shook her hand. "Thank you for getting your husband's attention for me." I laughed. "And I'm glad no harm came to you in doing so." Turning to shake the man's hand, I smiled. "My name is Olivia Harper."

"We know who you are," he said. "I'm Ben Fields. And my wife's name is Marsha. Now, what is this about?" he asked, his voice sounding strained.

Marsha huffed. "Don't be rude, old man." She smiled at me. "Would you like to come in? Or we can chat on the porch."

"Your lovely porch is fine. Thank you."

She rubbed her hands together. "I'll go make us some tea."

"That isn't necessary but thank you."

Marsha batted the air. "Oh, I insist. And you and Ben can take a seat."

She scurried in, her wide hips teetering with each limped step.

With a sigh, Ben plopped into one of the chairs. "Sorry. My wife can be quite bull-headed. Have a seat, Ms. Harper."

Ben was a nice looking, late middle-aged man, with a full head of salt and pepper hair and mossy green eyes. His trimmed goatee held hints of former auburn whiskers.

I smiled. "This is a lovely home, Mr. Fields."

"Call me Ben. I wouldn't have picked this particular style of home. But happy wife, happy life."

"How long have you lived here?"

"One year as of next month."

"Do you mind if I ask you a few more questions? I'm here because of a letter the Sparrow Haven police station received. If you don't have time now, I can have a detective come by some other time, or you can go to the station if you'd prefer."

His face blossomed with color. "I don't understand. I didn't write any letter."

I took the statement as a cue to open my notebook. "Do you mind if I take some notes?"

"Take notes about what?" he asked, his tone agitated.

"I'm here to discuss the investigation surrounding the murder of Victoria Thorne."

Ben's brow creased as he cackled. "You've got to be kidding me. This is absurd."

Just then, Marsha came back out. "Some warm oolong tea for us," she said, setting down the prepared tea tray. "And I'll be right back," she said, patting me on my shoulder. "Help yourself. There's vanilla or hazelnut cream and honey or sugar."

Smiling, I nodded. "Thanks."

Ben crossed his arms. "Are you questioning everyone who knew Victoria?"

Marsha came back out and placed a tray of tea cakes on the table before taking a seat in the rocker across from us.

I shook my head. "No, not everyone who knew her. I'm here because someone wrote a letter and sent it to the station, as I said before, and they mentioned your name in it."

"Who wrote the letter?"

"The letter does not have a signature."

Marsha grunted. "I'm willing to bet Linda Mills wrote it."

Ben shot her a glare and spoke through clenched teeth. "Shut your mouth, woman."

"I will do no such thing. You tell this lovely lady what you did, or I will."

Ben pounded the table with his fist, making the tea set shake. "That matter has nothing to do with this, Marsha. Don't you have something to go clean?"

She sunk her teeth into a white-frosted cake. "Nope." She turned to look at me. "Only a few people in Sparrow Haven know that the Thornes were our closest neighbors when we lived in Ballentine. Linda Mills knows this fact because my cheating husband had an affair with her...for two years."

Ben groaned. "And my wife stays to torment me for the rest of my life."

Marsha studied her next bite. "I try my best."

Shifting in my seat, I cleared my throat. "What did you and Victoria have a feud about?"

Ben rubbed his neck. "I...don't remember. The argument took place over a year ago."

"Liar," Marsha spat. "Ben here thinks Victoria killed our dog. It's the reason we moved. I chose Sparrow Haven for one reason. My sister lives here."

"Can you explain what your wife is talking about, Ben? Regarding your pet?"

"Ginger, our eight-year-old cocker spaniel, dealt with separation anxiety. She'd bark anytime we left the house. Victoria often complained about the noise. One day, Ginger mysteriously got out of the fence. Two days later, Victoria brought her home, claiming she'd found our dog roaming around town. Out of the blue, Ginger died the same day Victoria returned her to us."

"Just come out and say it, old man. He thinks Victoria poisoned Ginger."

"And you don't?" I asked.

"There's no denying Victoria had a mean streak the size of New England. But she wasn't evil. And only an evil person would do such a thing. So, no."

Ben harrumphed. "Marsha, do you think you know everything about everyone?"

"No, clearly I don't. Or I would have caught you cheating on me."

This interview was uncomfortable, and Marsha was making it difficult for me to keep the questioning on track. She had been helpful, but I needed to get Ben alone.

"Ben, would you mind showing me around your property? I'd love to get a better look at those bigleaf hydrangeas."

He abruptly stood. "Of course."

I followed him down the steps then fell in stride alongside of him. To my relief, Marsha went back to her rocker after picking up two more cakes.

Ben turned the water hose on. "I'd leave Marsha, but she would take everything I've worked my whole life for. I'm sorry you had to hear all that," he added, heading to the large purple flowers.

"No worries," I said, picking up the middle of the hose and following him. "May I ask if you went to the fair the day of the tasting?"

Ben placed a finger over the mouth of the hose to make the draining water spread wide. "Yeah, I've been at the fair most days. I run a concession stand and have done so for the last five years. I set up my booth at other events as well. It's my way to escape."

"What do you sell?"

"Simple stuff. Popcorn, cotton candy, and lemonade, mostly."

"Nice. So, did you see Victoria the day of the chowder tasting?"

He pointed the spray at the next bush. "No, I didn't see her. My slot is located on the opposite side of the fairgrounds. Near the Ferris wheel."

I wondered if Ethan had purchased our lemonades from Ben's concession stand.

"Do you run the stand alone, or do you hire help?"

"Just me, myself, and I."

"Do you think Victoria poisoned your dog?"

"Uh...no."

"Was the argument you and Victoria had a year ago about Ginger's death?"

"Uh...yes. But you need to understand. I'd just lost my baby unexpectedly. I was upset and needed to vent. Victoria was on the receiving end of it."

"Did you accuse Victoria of killing your dog?"

"I didn't come out and say it in so many words, but I did tell her it seemed a very odd coincidence."

"So, did you consider having the vet pathologist do an autopsy?"

There was a pause.

"No...Look, I didn't harm a hair on Victoria's head. We left Ballentine to get away from her. If I had planned to kill her, I would have done it a year ago, and I would have stayed in the town and home I grew up in. You have to believe me, Ms. Harper."

"I'm not here to accuse you of anything, only here to collect information."

"I understand," he said with a slight smile.

"Why would Linda Mills tell the police about the feud between you and Victoria?"

He cackled. "It's simple. Linda wanted me to leave my wife, and I didn't."

"Do you ever see Linda?"

"Not on purpose, but this is a small town. I don't think my wife wanted to move here to be near her sister. Marsha wanted my sin thrown in my face every now and again."

"Does your wife know Linda?"

"Yes. Linda owns a pet resort. We took Ginger there sometimes."

I glanced at my phone when it buzzed. Fred wanted me to call him. So, I thanked Ben for his time and asked him to thank Marsha for the tea before heading to my car.

Fred picked up on the first ring. "Hey, kiddo, about how awkward did the questioning get?"

I could feel his smirk through the phone. "So Linda told you about the affair with Ben?"

"Oh yes. Did Ben tell you why the affair ended?"

"No, I assumed it ended because his wife busted them."

"They didn't get busted. Linda Mills went to Ben's wife and told her about their two-year affair."

"Because she realized Ben would never leave his wife?"

"Not at all. Ben got physical during a drunken lover's quarrel. Linda says he pushed her to the ground and slapped her face. She told Marsha about the affair the same night."

"Does Linda really think Ben killed Victoria, or is this part of her revenge game?"

"Not sure. Tell me how things went on your end."

"Huh," Fred muttered after I'd finished telling him. "Linda told me about Ben's concession stand. He would use it as an excuse to leave home to go be with her."

"What a sneaky snake. Ben did admit being at the fair the day of the tasting."

"Yeah, Linda says he's been there every day. She's gone to check."

"She's a bit of a stalker, huh?"

"Oh, I definitely saw some crazy in her eyes. But with the Ginger bit, I'm not sure which way I'm leaning. But I know one thing. The limelight is quickly fading from your best friend"

9

—·—

Barkley and I walked down the sidewalk leading to Ethan's veterinary clinic, a familiar sight. The bell above the door tinkled softly as we stepped inside where we were greeted by the comforting scent of lemon mixed with a hint of sandalwood. The waiting area exuded a cozy charm, the walls adorned with framed photos of pets and their grateful owners.

We went to wait in a row of cushioned chairs, their upholstery displaying a subtle floral pattern. An old fireplace, its bricks painted white, rested opposite the seating area, giving the space a touch of old-world charm.

A few chairs down from us, a young couple nervously cradled a wriggling dachshund in their laps. Their worried eyes darted toward me, seeking solace in the presence of someone who understood their concern.

After asking which vet their pup would see today, I tried to encourage them by letting them know their puppy was in good hands. With Barkley sitting at my feet in rapt attention, I explained my dog's heart disease and told them how often we came here and about the good care he'd always received.

After Ethan's assistant called us back, they thanked me. It felt good to see their expressions less strained as I stood and bid them farewell.

The assistant motioned us back. "Hey, Olivia. Hey, Barkley." Leaning down, Angela ran her hand down his side. "How's my favorite boy been doing?"

"Spunky as ever," I answered. "He loves the new food you and Ethan suggested. And this diet seems to agree more with his digestive system," I added with a laugh.

Angela smiled. "That's always a good thing." She stood. "Any new concerns? Although I'm sure Ethan would already know."

"It's fine. I understand you still have to note Barkley's records. But no. He's all good."

She clasped her hands. "Wonderful. He'll be in shortly."

Just then, Ethan opened the door and entered.

Angela giggled. "Smart guy, not leaving your woman waiting."

Ethan smirked. "No, I was just anxious to see my favorite dog," he said, reaching down to pet Barkley, who was licking his hand.

After the door closed, Ethan gave me a kiss and a hug. "Thanks for waiting for me. I've been looking forward to helping work on the case with you today."

"And I look forward to having your help. I'll have to catch you up on everything on the way to Ballentine."

"I'm glad to hear the ball is rolling. Bet Milly is too," he added, while examining my dog's eyes and ears.

I shook my head. "Oh, Milly was ready to celebrate the other night after we ran into a new lead. I mean, she literally wanted to party like—"

"It's 1999?"

I laughed. "No, silly. Like we'd arrested the killer. I couldn't believe it."

Ethan checked Barkley's temperature. "Stress can do strange things to people. I can't imagine being a prime suspect in a murder case."

"Yeah, well. She's not cleared yet, but she's not considered a prime suspect anymore. We have suspects with clear motive now."

"Can't wait to hear more. Hey, I'm going to collect a blood sample before we leave, okay?"

My eyes widened. "Why? Did you find something concerning?"

Ethan came over and put his arm around me. "No, not at all. It's been six months, is all. Remember? I told you we'd do this."

"You promise?"

"Olivia. Come on. I wouldn't keep anything from you."

I just nodded.

Barkley didn't complain at all while Ethan collected the sample.

"Alright, I'll take this to the lab in the back, and I'll meet you at the car."

A few minutes later, we were headed to Ballentine, under a darkening sky. I was glad Angela had asked to take Barkley home to play. Her black lab and Barkley enjoyed playing together, and her offer saved us from needing to take him home first.

As we began our journey toward Ballentine, Ethan rolled his window down, allowing the wind to blow in the smell of pine and wildflowers. The road wound through the picturesque countryside, offering a glimpse of charming farmhouses and red barns nestled among the rolling hills. Fields of wildflowers swayed in the wind, creating waves of color stretching as far as the eye could see. A meandering river reflected the gray sky.

I usually preferred sunny days, but for some reason, the graying sky brought a sense of solitude to my soul. Perhaps it was because within an hour, I'd be questioning a woman who already carried the heavy burden of cancer. The wind picked up, rustling the leaves with a sense of urgency, as if nature itself was preparing for this difficult moment.

Ethan closed his window and studied me. "What's wrong?"

"I just…I'm not looking forward to questioning a woman about a murder when she's in the middle of fighting for her life. It feels wrong."

He squeezed my shoulder. "But it's not. This is the job. It's tough, I know. But this interview is necessary."

I sighed. "Yeah, I keep telling myself the same thing."

"I'll take you somewhere nice for dinner afterward."

I sent him a playful glare. "You think food holds some kind of healing power."

He chuckled. "I'm not the only one. You ever heard of comfort food?"

"Of course."

"Well, what do you consider comfort food?"

I smirked. "Anything that makes you fat by simply looking at it."

He laughed. "Sounds like we'll be hitting a fast-food joint then. I was hoping to wine and dine you."

"No, I'm not talking Big Mac. I'm talking about gourmet pizza. But Milly and I have been binge eating too much lately."

"Alright, well, you update me on the case, and I'll keep an eye out for somewhere good to eat."

I told him about the interview with Ben and his wife and about the conversation on the hot-air balloon ride. Also, I told him what Fred had gathered from Ben's mistress.

Ethan did a low whistle. "Wow. The suspect list has really grown. Can you brief me on the names?"

"Sure. So, we have the two clam chowder chefs, Antonio Gomez and Nancy Silverton. Then, Victoria's husband, Richard Thorne."

"I hope Milly doesn't know that Richard is a suspect."

"Oh, heck no. I haven't told her any specifics."

Ethan blew a fallen curl from his eyebrow. "Doesn't Milly know that the spouse is always initially a suspect? Oh, but you said she's not thinking clearly."

"Exactly. So, anyway. The other primary names on the list are obviously Ben Fields and who we are headed to see now—"

"Cathy Simons."

"And of course, anybody who is connected with the suspect is a person of interest."

"But mainly who falls in this category?"

"Well, Cathy's daughter, Monica. Ben's wife, Marsha, and his mistress, Linda. Then, Antonio's wife, Nina."

"What about the other chef, Nancy Silverton? No person of interest linked to her?"

"I mean, not that Fred has mentioned. To your point, the list has grown enough as it is."

***

As Ethan and I wound our way along the narrow mountain road, tall pines and maples closed in around us, the pitter-patter of light raindrops helping to calm my nerves. In their place, a determination built in my chest as each twist and turn brought us closer to our destination.

As we rounded the last bend, we came upon an old log cabin. The brown wood stain was faded from years of harsh conditions. As clouds broke, a few shimmers of early evening sunlight bathed the structure in a warm golden hue. Under different circumstances, the windows' glinting dance would have shown like welcoming beacons.

I eased the car to a stop on the gravel driveway, and we both stepped out, stretching our limbs after the hour and twenty minutes on the road. The air was cooler up here, and I pulled my jacket tighter around me, admiring the mountains stretching upward, their slopes dressed in a patchwork of vibrant greens and browns.

Ethan knocked, though we already heard the creaking steps of someone coming to the door.

The door opened, and I cringed slightly at the shocked face of Monica. Her expression matched the one I'd seen on the hot-air balloon ride.

I cleared my throat, hoping my voice would sound steady. "I'm sorry, Monica. But we need to speak with your mother. I promise to make this as brief as possible."

"How dare you come here? And I'm not sorry, but you will have to come back. My mother is sleeping, and I have no intentions of waking her up for this unnecessary visit."

A soft voice from inside the cabin spoke. "It's fine. Let them in, Monica."

She turned away from us. "But Mother—"

"Now, Monica Christine."

She glared but opened the door further before walking off.

Entering, I allowed my eyes to adjust to the image of a frail-looking woman wearing a nightgown, shaking as she attempted to sit up. Monica rushed over to assist her.

Once she had Cathy situated, Monica turned to us. "You might as well take a seat," she spat, waving her hand toward the two quilt-covered armchairs.

"Thank you," Ethan and I said in unison, before making introductions.

Monica pointed at her mother. "As you can see, my mother is bedridden. Do you actually think the weak woman before you is capable of waltzing into the fairgrounds to poison Victoria Thorne?"

Cathy Mills shushed her daughter. "Please ignore Monica. She's been overly protective since my diagnosis." She took a sip of water. "I'm sick for a few days after the treatment. Don't let my daughter fool you. I don't allow my condition to dictate my life. You can't keep a good woman down," she added, lightly laughing.

The fact that Cathy felt inclined to correct her daughter boded well for her. A bedridden condition could have worked as a solid alibi. Since Monica had attempted to cover this up with misleading information, this drastically changed my approach. My aim became to rattle Monica up even further than she already was.

So, I talked as if she wasn't here. "I think it's the gesture of a good daughter to be overprotective of her mother. Monica seems to be very distraught about the way Victoria closed down the tavern you owned."

Monica cursed. "Oh, now you're pointing the finger at me? Kiss my—"

"Enough," Cathy muttered, before looking back at me. "Yes. She's never gotten over it. Losing the tavern changed the course of both our lives. But Monica's most of all. She had to put herself through school to become an aeronautic engineer." She sent a proud smile to Monica. "But she did it, and I'm so proud."

"I'm sure her father is, too," I said, fishing for information.

Cathy shook her head. "I never married him or anyone else. It's been me and Monica against the world our whole lives. But we're both stronger than an ox because of it."

Monica stood up and crossed her arms, steam practically spewing from her nostrils. "I know what you're doing, Olivia. But I didn't do it. I was four hundred feet up at the time, and my site is located nowhere near the fairgrounds, as you well know."

My brow rose. "Yes, that is good to know. And I'm sure you have a copy of the passenger's receipt?"

"Of course, I do."

I genuinely smiled. "Oh, great. Would you mind sending me all of Monday's transactions?"

"No, I won't, for the privacy of my clients."

"That's fine. I'll just ask Detective O'Malley to obtain a warrant."

Cathy groaned, her face turning hard as stone. "Get off of our property. Right. Now. Unless you want to be on the wrong end of a gun." She glanced toward a shelved rifle.

Clearly, the defensive mama bear was making an appearance. We didn't stick around long enough to find out if she'd put action behind her threat or not. But, by the venomous look in Cathy's eyes, she'd meant every word.

10

—·—

As I approached my library, I couldn't help but feel a surge of pride. Its timeless charm of brick façade stood tall and dignified on the edge of Main Street. Ivy vines climbed the walls, their leaves a lush contrast against the stone.

Pushing open the heavy wooden door, I noticed that the air carried the familiar, comforting scent of aged books and polished wood. Only the occasional rustle of pages or the faint tapping of keys from the computer area broke the hushed atmosphere.

I made my way to the circulation desk, where Rose, my assistant I'd hired a couple of months ago, greeted me with a warm smile.

"You almost lasted a whole week without checking in," she said, giggling. "I'm proud of you." Playfully grinning, her full cheeks rose to her lower eyelids.

I smiled back and looked around to see the library in perfect shape. "There wasn't a need to come. The place has been in capable hands."

She winked. "Aw, thanks. It's been nice to keep busy since my boys started back at school. And you've been busier than a crushed anthill, I bet."

I tightened my ponytail. "Yes, and there's that."

"Making any headway?" she asked.

"Yes, thank goodness."

"I'm sure Milly is relieved, then."

"She's feeling optimistic. Finally."

"Poor thing. Milly is so sweet. I've been worried."

I nodded. "Thank you for holding the fort down. How's your week been?"

"Kind of dead, actually."

"It usually is when the fair is in town. Next week will probably be the same."

"Why don't you take next week off, then? I'm sure you'll be distracted with all you have going on. And you know I love playing boss around here."

My head tilted. "I just might take you up on that."

She rolled her eyes. "Not might. Say you will and promise to clear Milly's name by the end of the week. Besides, I'm sure you can't think about anything else."

"That's true." I headed over to the coffee area, Rose following my prompt.

"I could use another cup myself," she said.

I filled two cups, savoring the steam's salted-caramel aroma. Handing Rose a cup, I took a sip.

She made a sour face. "How do you drink coffee plain?" she asked, piling several sugar cubes into the brew before adding vanilla-flavored cream with a sprinkle of cinnamon.

Smiling, I pointed as she took a test-sip. "I can drink it plain because I actually like coffee, and you like caffeinated, liquid dessert."

Rose added two more sugar cubes. "That's not true," she said, winking.

I gazed about the room. "So, nobody's been here asking for me? Or—"

Rose snapped her fingers. "I'm glad you asked. Somebody came by and gave me a shoe box to give you. And I swear I heard and felt something move around inside."

I didn't take the last statement too seriously. Rose worked like a whiz at library duties, but she tended to be on the airheaded side otherwise. I liked to tease her, and we laughed often while working together.

"You heard something moving in the shoebox? Maybe there's dancing shoes inside," I said, smirking. "Why didn't you open the box to find out?"

Rose huffed. "Ha-ha. I didn't open it because the blasted thing freaked me out. So, I hid it away."

I laughed. "You hid a shoebox? Do I get to go find it?"

"Shush and follow me. I hope whatever it is didn't die."

I rolled my eyes. "I can't believe you didn't open the box."

"The woman who brought it made me promise not to. Besides, I stopped opening presents that didn't belong to me last Christmas," she sarcastically added.

I stopped in my tracks. "When did she leave it, and what did the woman look like?"

"You know I can't handle two questions at once, Olivia."

I spoke slowly. "Right. When did the woman bring it here?"

"Two days ago." Her chin lifted. "And she was wearing a floral, knee-length dress," she added proudly.

I sniffed. "The next question is, what did she look like? Not what was she wearing, Rose."

She batted at me. "I know. I was joking."

"Of course you were."

"The woman's description..." She huffed. "Dang it, Olivia. She had two eyes, a nose, and a mouth. It was two days ago for crying out loud! I don't have a photographic memory."

I chuckled. "Clearly. So, I'm looking for an ear-less woman. Perfect," I said, winking. "Would you mind fetching it, please? I'll be in the storage area."

"Good. Because that's where I hid it."

I sweetly smiled. "Brilliant. That's where I'd hide a shoebox," I kidded.

I followed her lead, and we entered the overstock area, and Rose began tapping her chin and looking around. "Where did I—"

"For the love of—"

Rose giggled. "I'm kidding," she said, yanking the box from its hiding place and handing it to me.

Rose stood beside me, her eyes fixed on the box as though it held secrets too dangerous to unveil. Her nervous energy seemed to hang in the air. She passed me a pen.

I took the offered pen and slit the tape on each end. Extending my hand out, I carefully lifted the lid, revealing its hidden contents. My heart raced once I peered inside at the sight of a snake with ominous markings. Its triangle head and vivid colors sent a shiver down my spine.

Rose's gasp next to me was a mirror of my shock.

The snake's unblinking gaze met mine, its forked tongue flickering out as it sensed the air. The following seconds felt like slow motion as I slammed the lid back down.

"Tape!" I squealed.

Rose ran to the shelf and tore a piece off. Then another.

"Oh my gosh, Olivia. I cannot believe this! What kind of snake is it?"

"I'm pretty sure it's a copperhead. Thank God you didn't open it, Rose."

"See? Never doubt your intuition."

"Did the woman check out any books, by any chance?" I laughed for even asking.

"No."

"Think hard, Rose. What color was her hair?"

She pinched the bridge of her nose, then snapped. "I don't know, because she wore a bandana."

My eyes narrowed. "What type of bandana?"

"It was elegant, made of satin, I believe. And vintage-styled."

"Let's get back to the floor," I said, before asking, "Did she look pale or sickly?"

"No. The lady looked fine, and I'd guess she was in her mid-fifties."

"Good. What else? Anything will help."

"I'm sorry. I was busy shelving books when she came in, so I didn't notice much."

Just then, a member walked toward the check-out desk, so I waited, trying to act casual by sipping on my coffee while glancing at the box on the counter. It felt eerie knowing what danger resided within it.

Rose swept her hands back and forth as if the book she'd handled had been dusty. "Okay, where were we?"

I smirked. "Going nowhere."

"Oh, dear. I'm sorry, Olivia."

"There is nothing to be sorry about. You were doing your job, and I appreciate everything you do, Rose."

"But I wish I knew more information. She literally tried to kill you!"

"Or she aimed to scare me off of the investigation. I know she made you promise not to open it, but did she say anything else?"

"Um, yes. She said to give you this message."

I waited for a moment.

"Can I assume she meant the snake? Or do you have a message to give me?"

She cackled. "No, silly. The snake is the message."

"Tell me how she said it, then."

"She said...someone asked me to deliver this message to Olivia Harper."

"I see. Well, that certainly changes things."

Rose looked delighted. "Oh, good. I'm glad I finally helped."

And I was glad I finally asked the right question. If someone else asked the woman to bring me the message, then she obviously knew the messenger and, most likely, the perpetrator.

Rose glanced down at the box. "What are you going to do with the snake?"

"I don't know. I guess it could go in one of the snake exhibits at Herb's aquarium."

"Good idea. So, you taking next week off?"

"No. But I may work half days, depending on the case. Sometimes distractions are a good thing, and they keep my mind fresh, too."

She nodded. "I understand. I do the same when I'm stuck with my writing."

My brow lifted. "What kind of stuff do you write?" I asked.

Rose batted the air. "Nothing too serious like mysteries or fantasy. I just dally in poetry and short stories."

"Oh, I'd love to read some of your work sometime." I glanced at the time. "See you on Monday. I'll plan to work from open to noon if that works for you?"

"Perfect. And if you need additional time off, just say the word. I can work whenever."

"Thanks so much," I said, glancing at a new text from Fred.

On the way back to my car, I called him.

"Hey, kiddo."

"Hey, Fred." I skipped small talk. "You'll never guess what I'm carrying."

"Okay, so then tell me."

"A shoebox. And you'll never guess what's inside," I said, to ruffle his feathers.

"Did you annoy your parents this much growing up?"

"Somebody put a venomous snake in a shoebox and brought it to the library. Of course, I wasn't there, so the woman handed it to Rose, made her promise not to open it, and told her to give it to me."

"What? Like a copperhead or a rattler?"

"I'm pretty sure it's a copperhead. Anyway, it was like pulling teeth finding this out, but the woman told Rose someone asked her to deliver this message to Olivia Harper."

A pause. "Well?"

I laughed. "Fred, the snake is the message."

"Well, why didn't you just say so? This is good, kiddo."

"Weird way to put it, but yeah. We must be getting close enough to be making someone extremely worried."

"Well, you sure are chipper. I'm glad you didn't get bit."

"Yeah, that would have been a day buster for sure."

Next, I told Fred about the visit to the cabin.

"Interesting. Yeah, I'll get to work on the warrant today."

"Okay. If it turns out Monica really was four hundred feet in the air at the time of the testing, we'll have one less suspect."

"That would be nice. At this point, I'm hoping this investigation will soon just be about the process of elimination."

"Did you have a chance to talk with Antonio's wife?"

He grunted. "Sure did. Little Nina is sweet as pie. I don't know how Antonio can treat her so badly. Anyway, Nina did know about Antonio's crush on Victoria. But she joked about it, as if her husband's infatuation didn't bother her at all. Nina said her husband has always been a flirt. She knew about it when they got married."

"Gosh, how did you ask Nina about her husband treating her so mean?"

"Like, pretty much what you just said."

"Cute. And?"

"Nina said she doesn't notice Antonio mistreating her."

"I'm going to call BS on that."

"No, I can buy it. Oftentimes, women who are mistreated get used to it, to the point where other people notice the cruelty, but they don't see it themselves. Or they've never been treated any other way by the male gender, so they don't know any different."

"It becomes the norm. Dang. How sad."

"I see this situation all the time. So, you taking the snake to Herb?"

"Nah, thought I'd keep a copperhead as a pet."

"Smart butt. Make sure you bring the box to me after you're done, so we can check it for prints. And tell Herb I said hey and tell him he still owes me a beer."

I didn't have to ask why. Herb liked to collect parking tickets.

11

I TEXTED HERB TO let him know I'd be there in twenty minutes and to make sure he knew the purpose for my visit. He replied with an excited face emoji and said he'd meet me at the snake exhibit.

True to his word, Herb, my retired marine biologist buddy, stood at the heart of the exhibit. With weathered hands and a slightly creased face, his beige attire blended seamlessly with the environment that he and his team had meticulously crafted. His eyes held a spark of excitement as he spotted me. Herb pointed at a small, square window before sliding the frame up.

I was relieved the window was big enough for the box size and more relieved when he took the reptile out of my hands.

Safe outside the glass, I moved closer, watching as Herb's gloved hand gently lifted the lid of the box. I waited with anticipation to see its full length. Slowly, Herb's hand emerged, cupping the copperhead snake, its markings glowing like fiery embers against the dim surroundings.

As the snake uncoiled in his hands, I couldn't help but marvel at its grace, its powerful body weaving a dance of life and danger. Through a peephole, I could hear Herb's voice low and like a melodic hum. He informed me about the serpent's role in the ecosystem, and he spoke of their elusive nature, their vital place in the food chain, and their misunderstood reputation.

With practiced ease, Herb lowered the copperhead into the neighboring exhibit. The snake seemed to sense the shift in the environment, its forked tongue tasting the unfamiliar air. Its sleek body glided through the lush vegetation, its movements a mesmerizing blend of purpose and stealth.

As Herb emerged from the glass box, his eyes met mine and a knowing smile played at the corners of his mouth. This exhibit was not just a collection of creatures; it was a living testament to his lifelong passion for marine life and conservation.

"You brought me a beauty, Olivia." He laughed. "I bet you didn't think so the moment you lifted the lid to that shoebox."

I rolled my eyes. "It looked like the devil to me."

He patted my shoulder. "Well, rest assured, if the person responsible knows anything about this snake, I doubt they were trying to take you out. The symptoms of copperhead venom take anywhere from one to eight hours to start. Your snake is a one-footer, so you would have had time to get to a hospital. But boy, you'd feel like death before it was better."

"In any case, I'll take it as semi-good news. I'd rather someone threaten to kill me then going straight to the deed."

Herb clucked his tongue. "I hope the threats don't get worse, Olivia. This first one was aggressive enough."

I blew air between my lips. "Don't I know it?"

He laughed. "I would have given anything to see your expression when you saw what was inside."

"I'm sure you can imagine. Rose looked petrified. I'm sure I did too."

Rose had previously worked for Herb, and he'd recommended her for the librarian position.

"How's she working out? I thought I'd never see the day when you'd hire another assistant librarian."

"Really? Why?"

He smiled. "Ah, well, you like everything so-so."

"How do you mean?" I asked, straightening his lop-sided bowtie.

Herb pointed. "That's what I mean."

"Okay. Point taken," I said, laughing. "But it has thrilled me to have Rose. She's a hard worker, shares my passion for the library, and we poke fun at one another."

He chuckled. "She is a little goofy."

"No, she's a lot goofy."

"The good thing is, Rose knows it. And she has a great sense of humor about it too."

I nodded. "True. We have a great time together. She makes me laugh more, and I've needed some light-heartedness lately."

"I'll bet. How's sweet Milly?"

"Funny how everyone calls her sweet Milly," I said with a wink. "She's okay. Better now than at first."

He gave me a sideways hug. "Milly is smart. She knows the determination and talent of her best friend."

Herb checked his watch. "I have ten minutes. Want to get a quick snack?"

I nodded and fell along stride of him, heading to the snack lounge. Taking our seats, I chose a bag of popcorn, and he chose an ice-cream sandwich.

"Jeez, I wish I had your metabolism."

"Give me a break, skinny. You shouldn't torture yourself by clean eating all the time."

I tossed a piece of popcorn in my mouth. "You haven't seen what Milly and I have been eating lately."

"Good. It's okay to cheat now and then. So, Fred told me the preparator used crushed hemlock seeds as their poison of choice."

Chewing a mouthful of popcorn, I nodded.

"Hemlock is often mistaken for edible plants like wild carrots or parsley because of its similar appearance. And you know it doesn't take much to be lethal. Hemlock is infamous for its historical use as a method of execution. Historians believe hemlock to have been the poison used in the death sentence of Socrates."

"Wow, back in the fifth century BC, then."

"My little book worm is correct. So, you know about the Socratic method of questioning, then?"

"Sure. It's a form of dialectical inquiry aimed at uncovering deeper truths."

He rolled his hand in the air. "Go on."

I bit my lower lip. "The knowledge train stops there."

"I'm still impressed. So, they also knew Socrates for his contributions to epistemology—the study of knowledge, belief, and justification. Don't you find that ironic?"

"You think this is linked to the killer justifying their crime?"

He shrugged, biting into his melting sandwich. "It's probably a small chance, but it's food for thought."

I bit into a half-popped kernel, enjoying the crunch. "Or maybe there is something to the whole carrot thing."

"Sure, maybe. Hemlock could certainly be a rare poison known only to a few of the top leading culinary experts. Have any leads emerged from the two chefs Milly worked with?"

I rubbed the back of my neck. "We have leads and motives piling up in every direction. I find both to be overwhelming at times."

Herb stood and deposited his half-eaten treat into a trash bin.

"Oh, that's why you stay slim," I said, winking.

"Don't tell anyone," he said. "I need to head out but thank you for bringing me a new friend."

"I'd say anytime, but not in this instance. I'm glad to be rid of the reptile, so thank you."

He laughed. "Hey, Olivia. About feeling overwhelmed. Just remember the elephant."

Herb enjoyed telling me fun facts about animals. "What about the elephant?"

"You know, how do you eat it?"

I batted at the air. "And here I thought you'd tell me something interesting."

He tapped his chin. "Alright. Here you go, then. Elephants use infrasound, low-frequency vocalizations that are below the range of human hearing to communicate over long distances."

My mouth dropped open. "Now, that's what I'm talking about. Just...wow."

He slightly bowed. "Always a pleasure, dear."

***

Earlier in the week, Ethan had planned a cookout for this evening, with the purpose of introducing his buddy, Norman, and Milly to one another.

He had charged me with bringing the dessert, saying he wanted to take care of dinner and the beverages.

I loaded Barkley and the Indian pudding I'd made after returning from the aquarium. The dessert was well known throughout New

England, popular for its custardy texture. The pudding included cornmeal, molasses, milk, and cinnamon. I had baked the mixture until it became thick and golden before drizzling maple syrup over it. I'd packed a container of vanilla ice cream to serve with it as well. Since Ethan lived in my neighborhood, there was no concern of the frozen ice cream melting in the warm summer air.

Ethan was in his backyard, likely preparing the charcoal grill, when I arrived. Barkley ran ahead through the open gate to greet Ethan while I retrieved the dessert stuff from the trunk of my car and put the dish in the kitchen and the ice cream in the freezer.

There were two glasses of chilled Chardonnay on the picnic table. Coming out the back door, I saw that Ethan's yard was in its usual immaculate state. The focal point of this tranquil oasis was the inviting outdoor fireplace area and cozy sitting area around the stone hearth.

Ethan greeted me with a sweet, prolonged kiss before handing me one of the wine glasses.

He raised his own. "Let's toast, shall we?"

I did likewise. "Okay."

Ethan winked. "To our matchmaking. May Milly and Norman go together like peanut butter and jelly."

I laughed. "To our matchmaking," I said, clinking his glass. "What time are they meeting here?"

"I told Norman to get here promptly at seven. And Milly a quarter after. So, they wouldn't have an awkward introduction in the driveway."

My brow rose. "Smart, so you can introduce Norman to Milly. Just how many times have you set people up?" I asked, following him to the grill.

He scraped the grate, heat permeating from the hot coals. "Um, twice before."

"How did it go those times?" I took a sip of wine before throwing the ball Barkley brought to my feet.

"The first set up went semi-well. They became good friends, is all. The second round turned into a complete disaster. They couldn't stand one another from the start."

I frowned. "Oh, no. I hope we aren't headed to a catastrophe."

"Nah. If nothing else, we can all enjoy this amazing summer evening and a yummy dinner."

I unwrapped the butcher paper to take a peek. "Hmm, swordfish. Good choice. What can I do to help?"

"You already did your part. I've got this," he said, leaning down to kiss my forehead.

He sprinkled seasoning on a fresh veggie medley and put it on the sizzling grill. Just then, I caught movement out of my peripheral vision.

I turned my head to find Ethan's buddy entering through the back gate. One word could sum up my description of Norman—lumberjack. With blonde hair and a broad frame, he walked with leisure and confidence at the same time. If nothing else, Milly would have some eye candy to enjoy for the evening.

Ethan introduced us.

Norman's voice came out rich and deep. "Ethan, you didn't tell me Olivia was this beautiful."

I batted my hand. "Oh, well, not compared to Milly," I said, trying to divert his focus.

Norman smiled. "I can't wait to meet her. I heard you two go way back."

"Yeah, we were born three weeks apart. We've known each other our whole lives."

Excusing myself, I went inside and called Milly. "You almost here?"

"I'm five minutes away. Is Norman there?"

"Yep. I just met him. Apparently, my boyfriend has good taste in men, at least in the looks department. And he seems nice."

"Thank goodness. I would have googled him, but Ethan wouldn't give me his last name or tell me anything about him."

"Ethan knows you well enough to know your type."

"Yeah, it's the only reason I agreed to this. You brought Barkley, right?"

I laughed. "You're about to meet a dashing lumberjack, and you ask if Barkley is here?"

"You know I love that dog more than anything. And if things get awkward with Norman, I'll have an excuse to get away from him."

I huffed. "Where is your optimism?"

"I lost it about five dates back."

"How much worse can it get?"

"This is Milly you're talking to."

"Well, I have a good feeling about this evening."

Milly sighed. "Good because I'm here now."

12

As MILLY ENTERED THE backyard, Barkley ran to her, wagging his tail profusely, so she bent down to give him some love. I thought she'd done well in picking out her outfit. She'd chosen an A-line sundress with a bold floral pattern that reached her mid-thigh. Bright blue hoop earrings dangled from her ears, and she'd tied her auburn hair back with a sash of the same color, making her large, blue eyes pop in the sunlight.

I watched for Norman's reaction as his eyes lit up with apparent pleasure.

Heading toward the grill where we all stood, Milly spotted Norman, and I could see the relief on her face, her smile growing in delight.

Ethan and I exchanged a brief look of triumph before he placed the swordfish fillets on the sizzling grate.

Putting the tongs down, Ethan took a sip of wine. "Norman, this is Milly. Milly, this is Norman," he said, using his glass to point at each of them. "So glad you both could make it this evening."

Expecting Norman to extend his hand for a shake, he surprised me by giving Milly a brief, one-arm hug. "I'm happy to meet you. You look even lovelier than Ethan described."

He'd used a similar line on me, making me question his versatility in communication skills. Or perhaps Norman felt nervous, and I was being too hard with my expectations.

Milly cackled. "He did the same describing you," she said, batting her lashes.

Ethan laughed. "Apparently, I need to work on conveying my opinions of others." He flipped the fish. "Why don't you all take a seat? I'll have everything ready in a couple of minutes."

Norman motioned for us to go first, regaining a point. He poured Milly a glass and handed it to her from across the table, before pouring one for himself—another point. However, Norman had shown up empty-handed. Even a semi-classy guy would have brought a bottle of wine or some other choice of beverage—a point taken away.

I held a platter out for Ethan to deposit the grilled veggies on and took it to the table after going to collect a serving utensil.

As I set the veggies down on the table, I saw Norman take a swig from his glass, and I wondered if I'd imagined a slightly distasteful expression flashing across his face. If so, the burly man quickly recovered, smacking his lip with approval.

"So," Norman turned to Milly. "Ethan tells me you own an antique store. Congrats on such an accomplishment."

Milly flashed a bright smile. "Thanks. Ethan didn't tell me an inkling about you. What do you do for a living?"

He chuckled. "I'm sure Ethan wanted us to have some element of surprise this evening."

Milly's brow rose. "I'd say a blind date is surprise enough."

"This is a date?"

Her mouth dropped open before quickly closing back. "Well, I—"

Norman's head tilted back with laughter. "I'm kidding, Milly. I'm enjoying this date very much." He reached out and squeezed her hand.

"I own a business, too. I'm an arborist. My crew and I cut trees down for a living. Our job is harder than you probably think."

"Actually, I didn't think being an arborist is a simple job at all."

At this point, I had to stifle laughter for two reasons...This guy really *was* the lumberjack I thought he resembled. And he'd mistaken Milly for a numbskull. Point given and a big point taken. Of course, she knew the job required strategic planning.

Norman's brow rose. "Really? Sorry. It's just most people don't understand the expertise involved in safely and efficiently cutting trees down in tricky locations."

Ethan sent me a concerned look as he placed a platter of fish on the table. "Jeez, Norman. Five minutes in, and you're apologizing for something?"

Norman nervously laughed. "Maybe this is why I'm still single at almost forty."

I felt compelled to help smooth things over. "Well, I don't totally understand the complexity of your job, and I'm sure that's the case with most people."

Milly rolled her eyes, knowing my intent.

Ethan waved his hand over the feast. "Help yourself, everyone, and I'll be right back with another bottle of wine."

Norman scooped a fillet up with his hand. "Actually, do you have any beer? The wine is okay, but I'm more of a beer kind of guy."

Ethan gave a thumbs up, with no apparent sign of disapproval. Maybe it was a guy thing, but a point was taken all the same. Someone so picky should definitely have brought their own beverage.

Ethan returned, took a seat, and made his plate after handing the beer over. "How's the swordfish, Norman?"

"Really good, man. Next time, I'll have you all over. I make a mean clam chowder." He sent Milly a wink. "I've heard you do too."

Milly's face grew red, and I braced myself for what might come out of her mouth.

Norman held up a hand. "Whoa, is it too soon? Goodness. I'm so sorry, but Ethan told me Olivia cleared your name already."

My bestie's rage shifted from Norman to me. "Is that true, Olive?"

I ignored her question. "Why would you discuss the case with Norman? Or anyone, for that matter, Ethan?"

He shook his head. "I didn't discuss the case with anyone. But I wanted to set Norman's mind at ease since I planned to introduce them to one another this evening."

"You wanted to put *his* mind at ease?" Milly asked, her arms crossed. She looked back at me. "What about *my* mind?"

I rubbed the back of my neck, wondering how this evening could get any worse. "You know I can't discuss the investigation with you, Milly. But I did tell you Fred and I were making a solid headway. Remember?" I shot Ethan a glare. "Besides, until they arrest the per-petrator, nobody's name will be totally cleared."

Norman cleared his throat, holding his beer up. "Maybe we should change the subject. I didn't mean to cause an argument."

Milly huffed. "And what would you like to talk about, exactly?"

He shrugged. "How about...the way eighteenth-century artists in-corporated hidden symbols in their artwork? For instance, the way specific kinds of flowers conveyed secret sentiments."

Ethan nodded. "Milly, I should have told you already, but Norman is quite the history buff. His knowledge in antiques is impressive." He sighed. "It's one reason I thought you two would hit it off." Ethan glanced back and forth between me and Milly. "Can we please just start over?"

Milly stood. "No, this was a bad idea. My life is too complicated at the moment." She regarded Norman with disgust. "Apparently your mom didn't teach you any manners. And you're about as funny as a fart in church."

Surprisingly, Norman took a swig of beer before chuckling. "I don't know. A toot in church would crack anybody up."

I covered my mouth, trying not to smile, let alone bust out laughing.

Ethan went ahead and let loose, laughing his head off. "Oh my god. This evening…it's not going the way I'd imagined it at all." He laughed again. "Sorry, but I find your metaphor comical as well, Milly."

Norman laughed again. "See? He's right. You're funny, Milly, and I like you. And I hope you'll give me another chance."

Milly glanced at everyone, and a slow smile formed on her face. "Yeah, I guess it is pretty funny."

Ethan winked. "Have a seat, Milly, please. And just so you know, Norman offered a few times to bring beer. I told him not to and then forgot about it and served wine."

Norman sweetly smiled. "One more chance, please?"

Finally, Milly returned the smile, hesitantly. "Alright, if you promise to tell me more about those eighteenth-century artists?"

I figured at this point, Norman had a fighting chance. Milly loved to discuss historical topics. Soon, the two were absorbed in easy conversation.

After our meal, Ethan and I collected the dishes and went inside after denying their offer to help.

Once in the kitchen, I watched as Norman and Milly played with Barkley.

Ethan came up behind me and put his arms around my waist. "I shouldn't have said anything to Norman about the investigation. Will you forgive me?"

I squeezed his hands. "There's nothing to forgive. I would have said the same thing in your shoes. I'm sorry for getting on to you about it out there. So, will you forgive me?"

"I understand why you did, but of course." He chuckled. "I can't believe we made a comeback this evening. Talk about a rough start."

"To be fair to Milly...Norman did act quirky in the beginning."

Ethan nodded, putting the leftovers in some containers. "I agree, but he handled Milly's jab about his mom not teaching him manners."

"Well, because you explained the whole drink issue to us."

"No, I'm not talking about the drink mix-up. I'm talking about the mom comment she made. It was a mistake not telling Milly anything about the guy. As a kid, Norman grew up in and out of foster homes."

My hand flew to my forehead. "Oh, gosh. Milly is going to feel like a heel when she finds out." I sighed. "But I see your point. He handled the conversation with grace by not calling her out on it."

"Exactly. He focused on that silly metaphor instead."

"I still can't believe Norman made the clam chowder joke, though."

"I know. He's a little rough around the edges."

I shrugged. "And Milly can be crude, so maybe they will be fine."

"Even if they don't end up together, I think they could at least become good friends."

I listened to them laughing together outside. "I agree."

13

— · —

ON MONDAY, I ARRIVED at my library three hours before opening time. Rose had let me know the tree-shaped bookshelf I'd ordered weeks ago had finally arrived, and I was anxious to assemble the piece on the far wall adjacent to the fireplace.

I began by laying out all the pre-cut boards, brackets, and screws neatly on the floor. As I ran my fingers along the wooden surfaces, I appreciated the stunning array of patterns and colors lining the board. The shades were reminiscent of aged oak, with subtle variations in tone, which added character to each piece. The wood featured swirling knots and fine lines meandering across the smooth surface. Once assembled, these patterns would tell their own story of the tree's growth over many decades, capturing the essence of strength and endurance.

The main trunk of the bookshelf showcased the oak's vertical grain, and as the branches branched out, they'd cut the boards in a way that allowed the grain to flow horizontally, emphasizing the natural, organic feel.

With a sense of purpose, I attached the brackets to the main trunk of the tree, ensuring everything was level and secure.

As the bookshelf took shape, a feeling of satisfaction washed over me. The shelves curved gracefully, resembling the branches of a mighty tree, giving my library an enchanting aura. I knew this would become the centerpiece of my library—a unique and functional piece that mirrored my passion for both literature and fine craftsmanship.

Securing the last branch, I stood back and marveled at the remarkable transformation the library had forgone. The unique shelf stretched across most of the wall, and now it was time for the most exciting part.

First, I reached for a collection of classic literature, carefully placing works by authors like Jane Austen, Charles Dickens, and Leo Tolstoy on the lower branches. These timeless stories had been my companions for years, and I wanted them easily accessible for my members.

Next came the non-fiction books, where I first included a diverse array of books covering art history, their covers adorned with famous paintings. Then, I placed books about natural history and the wonders of the natural world.

Finally, I reached for a specially bound, leather-covered book, a most cherished possession. In essence, the book was a family heirloom filled with handwritten recipes passed down through the generations. This book found its place on one of the uppermost branches, symbolizing the importance of heritage and tradition in my life.

I glanced at the grandfather clock and noticed that I only had ten minutes to spare. So, I brewed a fresh pot of coffee and enjoyed the new view with pride between each savory sip.

Just like the week before, members trickled in now and then, allowing me the time I needed to catch up on my time off last week.

I headed to the front door to lock up for lunch just as Rose arrived.

She spotted our new addition and gasped. "You did that by yourself?"

"Yeah, I've always been pretty good at assembling things. The company did an excellent job at writing the directions, and the task was really just about putting up the branches in the right order."

She shook her head. "Man, Olivia. It's just beautiful and adds such depth to the library. Well done."

"Thanks. Want me to bring you back anything from Vivi's café? I'm headed there now."

"Don't tempt me. I've already eaten lunch but thank you for offering. Hey, what did Herb have to say about that awful snake? I still get shivers when I think about it."

I squeezed her shoulder. "He gave good news. The copperhead's venom is treatable, and if it had struck me, I would have had plenty of time to get treated for it."

"I'm not so sure it is good news. What if the person didn't know? I certainly would have thought that horrible thing would have been fatal."

"I can't know for sure, but there is no point in thinking the worst. We're both fine, and that's what matters, Rose."

She glanced toward a window. "It's starting to rain." She held out an umbrella.

"I'm not going to take your umbrella. It's fine." I followed her gaze. "Oh, it's barely a drizzle. Have a good day and let me know if you need anything."

"You too. Are you meeting anyone at the café?"

"Detective O'Malley."

Rose made a sour face. "He's a grumpy thing, isn't he?"

I batted the air. "Don't let him fool you. He's all bark."

"Well, my boys are deathly afraid of him."

I laughed. "That's the way he wants it."

Hearing Rose lock the door behind me, I stepped out into the village, a light drizzle kissing my face. The scent of damp earth and fresh air filled the humid air. As always, I enjoyed passing the quaint shops and charming storefronts, their colorful awnings offering refuge from the rain.

Minutes later, I pushed open the café's door. A soothing wave of coolness and the aroma of spiced tea and freshly brewed coffee enveloped me. Vivi stood behind the counter, her infectious smile a ray of sunshine on the overcast day. Her fun, printed apron matched the sparkle in her dark brown eyes, and I admired her jet-black hair, which she'd pulled back into a stylish braid.

"Vivi, how are you?"

"Splendid. But just to warn you, Fred is in rare form."

My brow lifted. "Oh? He's in a good mood?"

She laughed. "Define good. He's at your usual table, dear. What can I bring you?"

"Do you have a new special for today?"

"Of course."

"I'll take it. Surprise me," I added with a wink.

Fred glanced up from his phone as I took a seat.

"You're ten minutes late."

I sent him a playful glare. "I walked in the rain to come see you. Give me some credit."

"And you didn't melt?"

I rolled my eyes. "Get up on the wrong side of the bed today, Fred?"

He grunted. "The missus asked me the same question."

"Your wife is an angel for putting up with you."

"Don't tell her. She might discover her wings and fly off." He took a huge bite of Vivi's popular Boston cream pie.

"Let's hope the dessert sweetens you up. Seriously, though. What's ailing you today?"

He grunted. "My team searched Monica's flight records. It's a dead end. A receipt verified her alibi."

"Monica could have made a false entry. Have they contacted the passengers for verification yet?"

"Yep. According to Detective Mccoy and Detective Harris, the flight is legit."

"Will you send me their findings?"

"You apparently haven't checked your email today," he said between chews.

Vivi placed a wrap on our table in front of me. "I know you love cranberries. And I chose fennel tea. This herb pairs well with turkey."

I picked up half of the cut wrap. "Hmm, a cranberry turkey wrap. Thank you, Vivi."

Glancing at Fred, she patted my shoulder. "Taking it easy on your faithful sleuth?"

"Not a chance. Have to keep her sharp."

Vivi giggled as she went to assist at another table.

Between bites, I told Fred about my visit with Herb at the aquarium. I passed him the box.

"He thinks a copperhead is nothing to worry about?"

I sipped on my tea, enjoying the liquid's warm, sweet undertone. "Well, the person could have chosen a more dangerous option. He did let me know later that it's rare to find a copperhead in this part of the United States. They're more common out West and in the Southeast."

Fred's mouth tilted downward. "Maybe the person is a snake collector, and they kept it in an aquarium?"

"Herb said if that is the case, they'd need to be an experienced individual who understands the snake's behavior and knows the protocols involved in owning one."

Fred crossed his arms. "It's illegal to keep venomous snakes as pets without the necessary permits."

"Yeah, I was about to say Herb told me as much."

"Well, I'll look into permits obtained. The record would stand out like a sore thumb, so my gut tells me the person obtained it from the illegal wildlife trade." He thought for a moment. "The snake could have come from Herb's aquarium, and you simply carried it back home."

My brow furrowed. "Herb would have mentioned this if it were a possibility. I could have been hurt. He wouldn't keep something like that to himself."

Fred sighed. "I know that, Olivia. But Herb focuses way more on the marine side of the aquarium. The place is so big now, there is no way he can keep up with every little insect or reptile. I'm saying it's something to consider."

"How serious are you about this scenario?"

"Serious enough to ask Herb for an employee list. We've got to start somewhere."

14

— • —

AFTER FRED AND I had finished up, I decided it was high time for Barkley and me to have some one-on-one time. Since I'd started dating Ethan, we didn't get much time by ourselves like we were used to. I simply wasn't ready to give up this part of my life—not yet and maybe not ever. Even if Ethan and I took our relationship to the next level, I'd need to find some moments to share with just me and my faithful companion.

As fate would have it, as I loaded Barkley and some of his toys up, Ethan called.

"Hey."

"Hi, beautiful. How did the meeting with Fred go?"

I put my car in drive and turned right onto the road. "Um, good, I guess. Fred wants to delve into where the copperhead could have come from."

"It's a smart idea. You can't find those kinds of snakes in your backyard around here."

Barkley could hear Ethan's voice, and he let out a single bark as if to say hello.

"Sounds like you and Barkley are driving somewhere."

"Yeah, I'm taking him to a dog park we haven't been to lately."

"Just the two of you, or is Milly going with you?"

"No, just me and Barkley."

"So, what did Norman think about Milly?"

"He's all about some Milly. What about her?"

"Milly wants to proceed with caution. But I can tell she's more excited than she lets on."

"With her record of duds, it's understandable."

"That's true," I said, laughing.

"I need to get back in. You and Barkley have fun."

"We will."

"I know. Call me later?"

"Of course, I'll call you later. I'm hoping to have some sort of update on the case," I added. "I'll need my assistant."

"Assistant?"

"Yes, do you have a problem with just being my assistant, Dr. Ethan?"

"It's not a problem as long as I'm spending time with you." He chuckled. "Olivia...I...nevermind"

I felt a little flutter in my belly. Was it just my imagination, or was he about to say those three big words?

***

The late afternoon sun hung lazily in the sky as we pulled up to the dog park. The warm rays cast a radiant hue across the vibrant green landscape.

We followed a winding trail through the woods, appreciating the scent of pine and wildflowers with each breeze.

Barkley's tail wagged like a metronome, setting the rhythm for our little adventure ahead. As we meandered along the pine-needled trail, the distant sounds of joyful barking and playful yips reached our ears, a cheerful symphony of canine delight.

We passed by a couple of families participating in dog events, including an exuberant game of fetch. A group of owners stood together, watching their dogs weaving through cones and leaping over.

Soon, the trail opened up, revealing the sprawling dog park ahead. Colorful picnic baskets, dog toys, and water bowls speckled the scene, and the air buzzed with the happy chatter of dog owners.

Barkley was off like a rocket, dashing toward a group of dogs engaged in a spirited game of tag. I watched him join the fray, his boundless energy and enthusiasm fitting right in with the canine camaraderie. With a smile, I settled onto a nearby bench in the warm embrace of the New England summer, content in the company of the dog-loving community gathered here today.

I jumped when someone suddenly spoke my name.

"Olivia Harper?"

"Yes?" I asked, turning my head toward the source.

It was a young man with coal-colored hair, sporting a Magnum P.I. mustache. He had the eyebrows to go with it. And the charming smile.

"May I?" he asked, pointing at the bench next to me.

"Of course."

"I'm glad the rain cleared. Though it made the day a bit humid." He looked at the bustling activity in the near distance. "Which one is yours?"

I pointed. "The golden retriever." I spotted two. "Mine is the darker of the two."

He laughed. "Mine is the lighter one."

I laughed too. "What a coincidence."

"Right? My dog's name is Clove. Yours?"

"Barkley."

He smirked. "Good one." He reached for a handshake. "Want to exchange human names while we're at it?"

My brow rose. "Apparently you know mine already."

He nodded. "Yes. Well, I'm Seth Silverton."

"Oh, does your middle name start with an S too?" I asked, kiddingly.

Seth chuckled. "It does, actually. But it sounds like SH. Any guesses?"

I tapped my chin, liking this young man already. "Sean?"

"So, you are as clever as everyone says. Yes, that's it."

"Are you by any chance related to the Chef Nancy Silverton?"

"Yes, again. Wow, beautiful and smart. Are you single?"

I laughed, feeling my cheeks burn at his bluntness. "I'm old, is what I am. Too old for you."

He swatted the air. "Age means nothing to me. Only beauty."

I cleared my throat. "I'm seeing someone, but I appreciate the compliment."

Seth sighed. "Figures. Listen, I came over here to thank you for clearing my mother's name."

Confused, I decided to tread lightly, hoping for insight. "Who did you hear that from?"

"My mother told me the murderer is in custody, but they haven't released the name yet."

Not knowing how to respond, I simply nodded.

"Have they told you who did it? Who poisoned Victoria?"

"I can't—"

"I understand." He smiled. "I'm just glad this is behind my mother. With her grudge against Victoria, I was really worried she'd be wrongly accused."

I kept my face neutral, thinking this didn't match Nancy's story.

"Well, it was a past grudge, so..."

He grunted. "My mother probably told you as much because she was scared. Believe me when I say she hated the woman's guts for publicly embarrassing her at an Italian tasting. My mother was the head chef at an Italian restaurant, Italian Dining Room, at the time. The owners blamed her for the temporary bad name it gave them. She's never really gotten back her good reputation."

"Your mom is lucky to have a son who cares so much."

At his point, I was pretty sure Nancy had told Seth a fib about them catching the killer, so her son wouldn't worry.

"I'm a mama's boy. My good-for-nothing dad left us after I was born. I can't believe she named me after that jerk. We've always taken care of each other."

"I'm glad you have each other. If someone asked your mother anything else about Victoria, what do you think she would say?"

"That's an easy one. She'd say Victoria lived to ruin anyone's life she thought to be inferior to her own."

"And you would agree with her?"

"One hundred percent. You know how the rumor mill works in this small town. I'd say a lot of people would agree. People were either hot or cold toward Victoria."

"So, let me make sure I understand. Are you saying people either loved her or hated her?"

Seth shrugged. "I'm sure there are a few neutral exceptions, but yes. That is what I was saying."

"And what category do you fall into?"

His brow furrowed. "You're smart. I think you know the answer already."

I kept my tone casual. "Well, you just said there were a few neutral people."

"I despise who my mother despises. We are on the same team." He stood up. "I need to get Clove and head out. But thanks again for all you do around here. And again, for clearing my mother."

Now, I felt a little guilty for playing the young man, though the questions were necessary.

"I...can't take credit for anything, Seth. Honestly, I hadn't heard about them catching the killer. But I'm not a police officer, so..."

His brow creased. "I'm confused. Everyone knows you're working the case with Detective O'Malley. That's true, right?"

I took a deep inhale. "Yes, I am. But again, I've not heard anything about what your mother told you."

He cursed. "Well, this is just great. Have you been baiting me?"

"Seth, you approached me and wanted to talk. And that's what we've been doing."

He groaned. "My mother can be such a liar when it comes to protecting me."

"I'm sure Nancy didn't want you to keep stressing about the investigation. My mom might have done the same thing in her shoes."

Seth shot me a glare. "You should have told me as much before now. Instead, you went along with it for information. I mean, you basically said the claim was true."

"No, if you remember, I asked you where you'd heard the claim from. But I'm sorry you're upset."

He shook his head. "Unbelievable."

I figured since Seth already disliked me, so I might as well ask the question. "Where were you the morning of the tasting?"

He put his hands on his hips. "I was at the fair with some friends. Does that make me the killer?"

"Of course not. But it places you near the scene of the crime."

"I could have lied. But there would be no point since I didn't commit any crime."

"Well, I appreciate your honesty, Seth."

He told me where to go and stormed away.

Shrugging it off, I entered a few notes into my phone. Then I called for Barkley, and we headed for a trail.

15

THE NEXT DAY, FRED and his team began working through the aquarium employee list provided by Herb. He also gave them access to review all camera footage throughout the facility. Both projects would take them days to sift through.

Fred granted Ethan and me permission to visit the tasting area of the fairgrounds, which they still had taped off for the ongoing investigation. I'd told Ethan I could meet him at the fairgrounds at half past noon.

The parking area adjacent to the fairgrounds was a sea of vehicles as families disembarked to immerse themselves in the festivities. Heading to the main entrance, I heard laughter and conversations dance on the breeze.

Fairground signage, with colorful graphics and whimsical fonts, promised games, attractions, and activities for all ages. The food stalls, a riot of flavors and aromas, continued to draw hungry crowds, the scent of fried dough and caramelized sugar tantalizing the senses.

I approached the Ferris wheel where I'd met Ethan the last time under drastically different circumstances. The iconic landmark stood tall against the sky, its spinning cabins carrying riders to new heights of excitement. Nearby, the amusement rides whirled and clanked, their colorful lights creating a dazzling spectacle in the daylight.

Scanning the vendor tents, staffed by artisans who proudly displayed their creations, I saw that they offered an array of handmade crafts, jewelry, and artwork.

My eyes followed a group of older kids who clutched their winnings from the game booths thus far. A couple of them broke away from the crowd that was heading to a dart game stand and skipped over to a lemonade booth instead; the same booth Ethan had ordered our drinks from the day of the tasting. And it was also the same one that Ben Fields owned and operated.

I fell in line behind the two boys who were giving their order to Ben. My mouth watered at the smell of freshly popped buttered popcorn wafting to my nose as Ben handed them a bag each.

"Can I get you anything else? Lemonade or bottled water, perhaps?" he asked them.

The boy glanced down at his credit card before declining.

I wouldn't want to eat popcorn without a drink, so I spoke up. "Hey, if you two want a drink, I'll buy it for you."

Their eyes lit up. "Really?" the shorter one said.

Acting like I hadn't noticed the way Ben's face had paled, I nodded. "Sure. Go ahead and tell him what you'd like to drink," I said, handing Ben my card.

Both boys requested a large lemonade. After Ben handed them the drinks, they thanked me and headed back to their friends.

Ben smiled. "That was very kind of you, Olivia."

I batted the air. "I wouldn't want to eat popcorn without a drink to wash it down."

"Would you like anything? It's on the house."

"Well, in that case, I'll take one of everything," I kidded.

He laughed. "Hungry, thirsty, or both?"

"Just two bottled waters please." I held out my card. "But only if you let me pay for them."

Ben nodded and took my card. "Who's the other water for?"

"My boyfriend should be here any minute. How have you been doing?"

He shrugged. "No point in complaining. I'm kind of surprised to see you at the fair, with what happened here and all," he added, handing me the bottles and my card.

"I'm here on assignment, actually."

"I see. Making sure the cops didn't overlook something at the crime scene?"

"A fresh set of eyes never hurts."

"And I suppose they aren't personally invested like you are."

"How do you mean?"

"Word has it you're trying to clear your best friend's name."

I twisted the cap off the bottle. "My focus is solely on finding the culprit."

I moved to the side, allowing Ben to assist a young couple waiting to order. After they'd gone, he rolled down the booth's shutter and stepped outside.

"Olivia, I understand your objective, but your childhood friend is a suspect. This connection makes you biased. Being a suspect myself...well, this troubles me. I've heard detectives sometimes pick a person to blame and then build a case around it."

"That doesn't happen in Sparrow Haven. We are following the same protocol and taking the same steps in solving this crime as we would in any other investigation."

I spotted Ethan heading our way, so I waved him over.

"Can I have a few more moments of your time? Alone?" I saw him glance towards Ethan. "I closed shop and came out here just to tell you something."

Within earshot, Ethan halted in his tracks. "Take your time, sir. I'll go get Olivia and me some lunch." He looked at me. "I'll meet you at the Greek food booth across the way. Sound good?"

I nodded. "A chicken gyro sounds good."

Giving me a thumbs up, he turned and walked off.

"What's on your mind, Ben?"

He motioned for me to follow him back into the booth. I didn't have any desire to be trapped with a man rumored to have a violent side. Ben must have picked up on my hesitation.

"I know about the false accusations about me, but you can trust me, Olivia. I'll even keep the door open. It's just so loud out here, and I need to focus on how to say what's on my mind."

I glanced around and spotted Ethan nearby. "Alright."

After we stepped inside, Ben offered me a seat on his stool before resting his elbows on the counter, blocking the doorway.

"Thanks, but I'm fine to stand."

He rubbed his stubbled chin. "You probably know this, but after you questioned me last week, the very next day, I allowed the cops to search this booth for evidence."

"Yes, I was aware."

"And they left empty-handed." His face turned to stone as his hand reached inside his pocket.

I took a step to the side, ready to push him and make a run for it.

"I'm not going to hurt you." Ben held a baggie toward me. "The very next day, I found this inside my booth. My guess is these dried leaves will match the poison used to kill Victoria." He nodded toward the bag. "Take the bag off my hands, please. I thought about turning it in, but I've been torn about what to do."

Taking the bag, I shook my head. "What do you mean?"

His eyes darkened. "My wife and former mistress planted the poison in here, thinking the cops hadn't searched the booth yet." He gruffly ran his hand through his disheveled hair. "I know for sure they are trying to set me up, Olivia. I even have footage of it." He took a step forward and firmly gripped my shoulders. "Listen to me carefully. I believe Marsha and Linda killed Victoria with the purpose of taking me down for the murder."

"Take your hands off of me, right now. Please."

Groaning, he shook me. "Don't you understand what this means?"

Just then, a muscular arm from behind wrapped around Ben's neck. "Release her. Right now."

Ben put surrendering hands in the air. "I'm sorry. I'm so sorry." He began sobbing. "I didn't realize what I was doing. Did I hurt you?"

I straightened my shirt. "I'm fine."

Desperation flowed from his eyes. "You have to stop them. I didn't want to tell you because they are the only two women I've ever loved. But what does it matter when they both hate me? And besides, I don't want an innocent person sent to prison for murder. I couldn't live with myself."

Ethan took my hand and led me out. Once there was distance between Ben and us, I turned and looked him straight in the eye.

I spoke low, hoping my voice wouldn't crack. "Thank you for the information, Ben. I'd advise you to go to the police station and file a police report."

"Okay. Should I take the bag of poison with me?"

"That won't be necessary. I will make sure the item gets put into evidence and tested. You have my word."

"Oh god, what have I done? Did I do the right thing?"

"If your story is true, then yes," I answered, and allowed Ethan to guide me away.

"Are you okay?" he asked, putting his arm around me.

"Yeah, I'm fine."

He titled my chin up. "Did he hurt you?"

"Not really. I'm fine, seriously."

"Why did you go inside with him?"

I rubbed my neck. "I made a bad call. It won't happen again. Thank you for showing up when you did."

"Well, when I couldn't see you, something told me to hightail it back over to you."

"Thank you, my rescuer," I said, trying to lighten the mood.

He kissed my cheek. "You're welcome. Are you still hungry?"

I glanced at the time. "I'll get something to eat after we leave here."

"I'm not hungry anymore, either."

I took his hand, and we made our way down the path toward the crime scene.

As we approached the tasting area, my heart quickened with a mix of curiosity and apprehension. The scene, once abuzz with the excitement of a tasting competition, now appeared serene and deceptively ordinary, as if it were trying to conceal the horrific moment that had unfolded just days ago.

Yellow crime scene tape crisscrossed the space, forming a barrier that marked the boundary of the investigation area. The once-bustling cook stations had been meticulously cleaned and cleared out, their gleaming surfaces devoid of any remnants of culinary creativity. The stage that had hosted the judge stood silent and eerily vacant. Empty tasting tables remained in orderly rows, but the memory of the chaos when Victoria fell ill before collapsing lingered in the air.

***

I doubted we'd find anything significant. Fred's team of forensic experts had scrutinized every inch of the area, but I'd been drawn back here for my own peace of mind.

Ethan and I exchanged a somber glance, our thoughts unspoken, yet both of us knew what the other was thinking about: how the former camaraderie had been transformed into a haunting tableau of a culinary murder.

The stall of interest was small, with a narrow serving area. There was one way in and out of the structure, by a doorless threshold at the back of the wooden box. I couldn't help but wonder how something so sinister could unfold in such a confined setting.

I shuffled my shoe around the dirt floor before going to stand in front of the serving area. "It's no wonder the person slipped in and out unnoticed."

"Yeah, and no wonder the team didn't find prints. They wouldn't have needed to touch anything."

"Not at all," I agreed. "The person came in hunched below view, poured the crushed hemlock seeds into the tasting pot and slipped out."

"Don't you think they would have stirred the contents into the chowder, though?"

"No, not if the person knew the tasting procedures. One of the cooks stirs the chowder just before the judge takes a bite. This ensures that the chowder is evenly heated and that the bite includes all the ingredients in the taste test."

"What was the poison potency when forensics tested the chowder?"

"Extremely high. Fred says they put seven times more hemlock than was even necessary to do the job. That's why the single bite killed Victoria so quickly."

"So, roughly, how much did the person pour in?"

"They estimate two tablespoons. The seeds were ground to a fine powder and its virtually colorless and odorless, so the stirrer wouldn't have noticed anything was amiss."

I joined Ethan at the back of the stall, and we both peered outside. In the distance, several yards back, we saw a narrow corridor leading to a small storage area. We went to it, but they'd locked the building. So, I used the camera on my phone and sent Milly a picture of the unit with a question mark below. She replied within seconds.

"Milly says we can get a key from the main office. We need to ask for..." I laughed. "Hairy Larry."

Ethan chuckled. "Alright then. Let's go find him."

I put my hand through Ethan's offered arm, and after studying a posted map of the fairgrounds, we headed toward the main office.

"Want to tell me why Ben Fields lost his mind earlier?"

I sent him a shy smile. "Of course." I showed Ethan the baggy of dried leaves. "He gave me this. Ben thinks his wife and former mistress are the killers, and they are setting him up. He claims they planted the so-called poison in his concession stand."

"They must not know the killer didn't use the leaf of the plant."

"No, only law enforcement and a select few know the killer used the seeds."

"Do you think it's the opposite? And Ben is actually trying to set the women up?"

I nodded. "If any of them are guilty, I would lean that way. Ben's wife can't stand him. I've seen her animosity toward him. And Linda sent a letter to the police station letting them know about the feud between Ben and Victoria."

"Well then, Linda is obviously pointing fingers."

"Yeah. Ben, Marsha, and Linda are definitely one big, triangular mess."

"So many of our suspects possess heavy motive. How can we start narrowing the list down?"

I sighed. "By taking it one suspect at a time. All while hoping that new leads emerge."

16

— · —

MILLY HADN'T BEEN EXAGGERATING when she'd nicknamed Larry. I opened the front office door just as he was about to walk outside and received an up close and personal view of his nostril hairs. And it didn't end there. The tall man with a beach ball-sized gut had hair growing out of every pore on his body.

"Are you Larry?" I asked, taking a couple of steps back.

His unibrow rose to meet long-curled eyebrows. "You're the gal from the newspapers. Olivia Harper, right?"

I shook his pudgy hand. "Yes. So, you're H...Larry?"

He laughed, making his gut bounce. "It's okay. Everyone calls me Hairy Larry." He proudly displayed both arms, which appeared skinless under the carpets of hair. "What can I do you for?"

I took the next moment to introduce Ethan.

"We were wondering if you'd grant us access to the storage facility located on the tasting grounds?"

Larry tugged on his braided beard. "Ah, for the murder case, right?"

"Yes," I answered, moving out of his path.

His large ring of keys jingled with every step. "I don't give out keys, but I'll walk you back and open the unit for you. How does that sound?"

"Great. Thank you."

As we journeyed behind the wake of dust Larry's large boots threw into the air, he reminisced about the past fairs of Sparrow Haven. He'd been employed for all of them going back ten years.

"We've had some accidental injuries over the years, but nothing like this. It makes me want to wring the neck of whoever did it, Ms. Harper. I thought our town is above things like this."

"You can call me Olivia."

His long hair swayed as he shook his head. "Are you sure? I have the utmost respect for your work. It would be weird for me to call you by your first name."

I smiled. "Well, it's weird for me to call you Hairy Larry."

His deep-throated laughter filled the air. "Alright, Olivia. You're even nicer than I'd imagined. How's that sweet Milly doing? I know she was close to Victoria, and for the murder to happen right under her nose..."

"It's been rough, but she's doing okay. Thanks for asking."

Larry groaned. "Actually, the murder happened right under all our noses," he said, unlocking the storage room. "I must've been standing about right here when the person poisoned the chowder. It makes me sick to think I could have done something about it."

My eyes grew wide. "What exactly did you see?"

He crossed his burly arms. "Well, Milly and I were chit-chatting when I saw someone enter their tasting stall out of the corner of my eye. I didn't think anything about it."

"Did you see what the person looked like?"

"I've never been real observant. The person could have been Ronald McDonald for all I know."

"So, you think you saw a man enter the stall?"

"Not at all what I'm saying. It also could have been Betty Boop."

"Maybe you saw Antonio or Nancy entering the stall, then?"

"Maybe. I'm pretty sure they were both inside here, though," he said, opening the door to the storage unit. "I mean, they were both inside when Milly and I started chatting it up, anyway."

"Do you remember if the three of them went back to the tasting stall together?"

Larry stretched his back, causing his vertebrae to obnoxiously crack. "Sorry, I don't. But something Chef Antonio said to me that morning stuck in my head. He made the statement right before him and Chef Nancy went inside here to get utensils." He motioned for us to follow him into the unit.

This was starting to feel like pulling teeth. "What did Antonio say?"

"Well, first you need to know what I asked them."

"Okay."

"I asked them what they thought their chances were for winning first place again."

"Alright."

"And Antonio said they were very confident. That they'd made up some killer chowder."

I kept my face neutral. "Anything else?"

He scratched his scruffy head. "No. I mean, Nancy agreed with him, but that's pretty much the gist."

"Was Milly present when Antonio made the comment?"

"Sure. But she was staring at her phone at the time."

I went to stand where Larry said he had been standing outside the unit. There was a clear visual of the back entrance to their tasting stall.

Larry leaned out, his frame taking up the entire doorway. "Told you I could see the killer enter the stall."

"I see what you mean. Sometimes taking a look helps me to see things for myself. Do you know how long the person was inside the tasting stall?"

"Not exactly, but it wasn't for long. Milly and I talked for just a few minutes, and they were obviously gone by the time she went back."

"You said that while you and Milly were talking, Nancy and Antonio were inside the storage building. You didn't see one of them leave during your conversation?"

"No, not that I noticed. Sorry. I feel like I'm not helping at all."

"No, no, this is all very helpful."

I rejoined Ethan inside the building, where shelves were stocked with various kitchen supplies along the corridor walls. Someone kept the place neatly organized. Labeled containers of spices, herbs, and seasonings lined one of the shelves, providing insight into the ingredients used by the chefs prior to the competition. At the far end of the storage area, a small refrigeration unit hummed softly. Opening it, I found the unit housed dairy products.

Larry spoke from behind. "They'll come clear all this out once the investigation is over. I figure they didn't tape this part off because I keep it locked."

"They searched this building, though, right?" Ethan asked.

"They did."

Crossing my arms, I studied my surroundings more carefully. The area resembled a treasure trove of culinary artifacts, where they'd displayed all kinds of kitchen supplies. As I ventured further into the unit, a glimmer of silver amidst the organized assortment drew my eyes.

There, in plain sight on a weathered wooden shelf, sat a small silver platter. Its surface had acquired a patina over the years, but the intricate patterns etched into the metal still hinted at its former elegance.

Slipping on a pair of gloves from my case, I reached out with wide-eyed astonishment. Upon the platter rested a stone mortar and pestle. Nestled beside the tool, they had placed dried flowers and seeds. The cluster emitted a strong, earthy aroma reminiscent of a meadow in bloom, which contrasted starkly with the sterile environment of the storage unit. Sniffing the tiny pile of seeds, I noticed that they offered a subtle nutty aroma.

The person had tucked a folded sticky note on the back of the tray. Using one finger, I pushed the folded flap down to find a typed note in bold print.

I read the words aloud. "'Catch me if you can, Harper.'"

"What the heck?" Ethan asked. "The killer knew you'd find this, Olivia. And they're toying with you."

"Apparently. They've handed me evidence on a silver platter. This is so bizarre."

I tilted the small stone bowl. A fine powdery substance layered the round parameter.

Ethan's brow furrowed. "Why would the killer hand over the murder weapon?"

I shook my head in bewilderment. "The killer must think this is some kind of game. Get me an evidence bag, please?" I asked, nearly breathless.

Larry grunted. "None of that was in here when the cops searched this place."

"Who else has a key to this building?" Ethan asked, handing me a bag.

His mouth bobbed open and shut before any words came out. "Far as I know, just management and a few employees."

"So, how many keys are there?"

"Five, I think."

I sealed the bag. "I'll need a list of names, Larry. And how long each of them has worked at the fairgrounds, please." I unlocked my phone and punched in the names as he stated them, none of which sounded familiar. "Do these people take their keys home? Or do they keep them in the office?"

He shrugged. "We pretty much keep them on a peg board in the manager's breakroom. I have been known to forget sometimes and bring them home. But it's not a big deal or anything."

"Is there anyone in particular who comes in here on a regular basis?" Ethan asked.

"No. We don't use this unit a lot. A few times a year is all."

"You said the staff keep the unit locked?" I asked.

"Yeah, because a few months back we found some kids using the place as a hang out."

Ethan shook Larry's hand, and we both thanked him for his time. I tucked the evidence inside my bag, and we headed back to our cars.

Ethan put his arm around me. "Fred isn't going to believe this."

I smiled up at him. "I know. I'm shocked too."

"How in the world did the killer know you'd be the one to find it?"

"I'm sure the person took a chance, thinking I'd possibly do my own search."

"Good point. Perhaps the killer follows your work and knew you'd eventually search the unit. I just hope they aren't following *you*."

17

As I DROVE TO the police station, Ethan's words kept replaying in my mind. I found myself looking in my rearview mirror every other minute to see if someone was following me.

Besides my bout of paranoia, the note's message had infused anger within my spirit, making me all the more determined to solve this case. The phrase written on the paper held a teasing tone, as if the person had no remorse for what they'd done. On the contrary, the person must be proud of the act and reveling in their freedom—a freedom I planned to take from them as soon as possible.

I pushed open the heavy glass door of the police station and was greeted with the sterile and slightly musty scent of the old building. The dull fluorescent lights overhead buzzed softly, casting a pallid glow over the white-tiled floor.

The station was quiet for the early evening hour. A few officers shuffled through paperwork at their desks, their conversations hushed and focused. The low rambling of a phone call emanated from a nearby cubicle, and the clatter of keyboards occasionally punctuated the otherwise subdued atmosphere.

I approached the front desk, where a uniformed officer sat behind a computer monitor, engrossed in typing a report. The muted sound of a police radio sitting on her desk intermittently cracked with updates and dispatches.

I cleared my throat so as not to startle her. "Hey, Tess. Is Fred in?"

"Hey, Olivia. Yeah, he was in his office last I checked. Otherwise, you know where to find him," she added with a wink.

I laughed. "I'll check his office first. Then the breakroom."

She smiled. "Bingo."

Just then, a commotion coming through the front door caught our attention. It was Ben Fields, Marsha, and Linda. They were screaming at the top of their lungs at one another, throwing out accusations and threats, charging the atmosphere with pent-up resentment and betrayal.

Marsha's hands balled into fists, her knuckles white with rage. Linda, equally incensed, reciprocated in kind. The room erupted into chaos as the two women, fueled by their emotions, began exchanging punches, their movements wild and uncontrolled.

Ben screamed curses, pushing them both so abruptly, the two women stumbled backwards into the glass door.

The cops nearest to the rampage ran over and detained them, slapping cuffs on their hands before leading them to individual holding cells.

So engrossed in the fight, I didn't see Fred exit his office.

"Bring a storm in with you, kiddo?" he asked, shaking his head and motioning for me to follow.

"Let's have a chat before we question the nut jobs, shall we?"

I chuckled. "I figured the crazy trio would make an appearance at some point, but I hadn't pictured the scene going quite like that."

"Well, the madness keeps life interesting around here for sure."

"Yeah, that's one way of putting it."

Taking a seat in front of his desk, I noticed a new portrait of Fred and his wife. "What a lovely photo. How's Mrs. O'Malley been doing?"

"Ornery as ever. She came in yesterday and replaced the picture in the frame. I guess she thinks I'll forget what she looks like otherwise."

"She has to be a little ornery to put up with your cranky butt. And the picture is probably to remind you to behave yourself, or you'll have her to answer to," I added, pointing to Mrs. O'Malley.

"It's her world. I just live in it."

I rolled my eyes, having seen first-hand how much Fred adored his thoughtful wife.

Fred tilted his head toward my crime case as he took a seat. "You only bring that in when you have something for me. So, out with it already."

I displayed the evidence and brought him up to speed about the storage unit.

Fred stood and leaned over the note. "'Catch me if you can, Harper.'"

"Crazy, right?"

"The person is boasting about the crime, thinking we'll never catch them."

"Have you ever had a killer hand over the weapon?"

He shook his head. "No, I'm shocked. Usually, only someone who intends to kill again starts a game like this."

My stomach hit the floor. "You think we have a serial killer on our hands?"

"I hope to God not. It's probably more likely we have a one-time murder, and the one-time murderer is basking in the glory of getting away with the act. Like I said, they don't think we have a fighting chance of catching them."

"Let them think as much. Their mindset is making them sloppy."

"Good job, kiddo. I'm proud of you."

I smiled. "For searching the storage unit?"

"Exactly. For re-searching it after we did. Seems the killer knew you would, too."

"Ethan said the same thing. Gives me an eerie feeling."

Fred shrugged. "Well, at least they didn't threaten you. On a different note, do you know anything new about the three idiots in the holding cells?"

"Yeah, as of today, actually." I retrieved the bag of dried leaves. "Ben thinks Marsha and Linda planted this in his concession stand in hopes of framing him for the murder."

Fred cackled. "Based on what I just saw in the lobby, those two women despise each other too much to do anything together."

I shrugged. "Well, they do have one thing in common. They both hate Ben. I'm pretty certain neither of them is our killer, but..."

"I agree. But if one or both of the women aimed to frame Ben, he has every right to press charges."

We took the evidence bags to the evidence room, and Fred logged the entries in the system before handing them over to the forensic team. Next, we headed to the holding cells.

"Who should we talk to first?" I asked. "Ben?"

"Yeah, I was thinking the same."

I peered through the cold steel bars of the holding cell. Ben sat on a narrow bench, his posture rigid, his hands gripping his knees. His brow furrowed, and his eyes blazed with fierce intensity. Standing up, Ben regarded me with a tightly set jaw, and he pressed his lips into a thin line.

"Those women have lost their minds."

"Would Marsha and Linda say the same about you?" Fred asked.

"I couldn't care less what they think of me anymore. And to think I wanted to protect them."

Fred sighed as if bored. "Protect them from what?"

He waved his arms around. "From years in here. They planned to frame me for murder. Last I knew, conspiracy and false reporting were illegal."

"How do you know they planted the evidence in your concession stand?"

"I knew one or both of them were up to something. When you told me someone had sent a note to the station, I figured the writer had to be Linda, and I knew she wouldn't give up easily. On a hunch, I hid a camera in my concession stand. Come to find out, my wife was in on the framing too."

"And you have the footage to prove your claim?"

"Damn straight."

"Do they know about the footage?"

"They do now. I sent the video to their phones."

"What were the women fighting about out there?"

"They were arguing about whose idea it had been to plant the hemlock." He crossed his arms with a coy smile. "You better believe I'll be pressing charges. They both deserve what's coming to them."

"At the fair today, you were reluctant to file a police report. What changed?" I asked.

"Losing it the way I did with you earlier. I lost my self-control from feeling guilty about not coming forward. I decided I'd rather Marsha and Linda pay the consequences instead of me. I know they killed Victoria."

"You want to know what I think?" Fred asked. "I don't think any of you killed Victoria Thorne."

"Why not?"

"None of you know what part of the plant the killer used to poison her." Fred held the bag of dried leaves up. "This was not it."

"Neither one of those women is detail-oriented. It's hemlock, so point made."

"Well, that's the other thing. The perpetrator was extremely detail-oriented."

Ben glared. "Killers or not, I'm still going to press charges."

Fred shrugged. "Okay. Are you sure about that?"

Ben cursed, running his hand through his messy head of hair. "No, wait. I guess it's not worth the hassle. I don't need this kind of drama in my life."

Fred clasped his hands together. "Alright."

"But I want a restraining order against them."

Fred unlocked the cell, glancing behind him at the officer at the back of the room. "Officer Gomez will be happy to assist you with the order."

Next, we headed toward Ben's wife's cell.

As soon as she spotted us, she stood up and swiped at a falling tear. "Planting the hemlock was Linda's idea. Not mine. I only went along with it because I don't trust you two to solve the case. You should have by now. And I know for sure Ben killed Victoria."

"And how do you know this?" Fred asked, crossing his arms.

"Before we moved here, Ben told me he wished someone would poison her the way she poisoned Ginger."

"So what? Wishing isn't the same as doing."

She groaned. "He knew Victoria had lots of enemies. But when nobody did anything about it, he did the job himself. I'm sure of it. He's a violent man."

"And your proof?" I asked.

"I don't have any. So, do your job and prove what I'm telling you."

Fred unlocked the cell. "I recommend you stay clear of this investigation. And if you think your husband is capable of murder, perhaps stay clear of him as well. But whatever you do, don't come back here again."

"Fine, but I need a restraining order."

Fred grunted. "Seems to be going around today."

As we approached Linda, her face showed no emotion. Someone might think she'd been sitting on her couch instead of in a cell.

"Hey," Linda said. "Thanks for coming to talk with me. There's been a huge misunderstanding." She giggled. "It happens, right?"

"What happens?" Fred asked nonchalantly.

"Marsha said that if I didn't help frame Ben, she'd tell my family about our affair. You see, Marsha blackmailed me into conspiring against her husband."

"I think the letter you sent to the station says otherwise."

Her smile was overly sweet. "The letter was true. And you know it. Ben and Victoria did have a feud. I simply made you aware of it."

Fred held up the baggie of dried leaves. "Is this hemlock?"

"No, it's dandelion," she said, rolling her eyes. "Of course it's hemlock."

"Where did you find it?" he asked.

"How do you know I found it? Maybe Marsha found it."

"Tell me, or I'll arrest you for obstruction of justice."

Linda's mouth dropped open. "On what grounds?"

"On the grounds of I can. And I will."

"I googled where the plant grows. I found a colony of it growing along Sheldon Stream. Don't tell me you didn't know hemlock grows in New England?"

Fred apparently was done with this conversation. He unlocked the cell. "Get out of my station."

"You still have no idea who killed Victoria, do you?"

Fred pointed. "Out. Before I change my mind about letting you go."

18

— · —

COMING UP MY LONG driveway, I spotted a man sitting on the steps of my front porch. As I put my car in park, Richard Thorne stood and waved, holding a piece of paper in his hand.

Next, I spotted a car coming up my drive from my rearview mirror—Milly.

I sighed, wondering what had transpired to bring them to my home this evening. A heads-up from Milly would have been nice, but she knew I'd likely tell her not to come if this had anything to do with the case. And I couldn't think of any other reason the two of them would be here.

Richard met me halfway up my walkway. "Good evening, Olivia. I'm so sorry to barge in on your evening like this, but what I have couldn't wait. I have received something, and it's from the murderer..." He paused. "But perhaps I should have called first."

I smiled. "No, I'm glad you came, Richard." I looked over at Milly as she closed her car door. "But why are you here? You know I can't discuss—"

"So don't," she cut in, holding up a bag of groceries. "I'm just here to make us dinner while you and Richard talk. You're hungry, aren't you?"

"Yeah, and you're sneaky."

Richard held up a hand. "It's my fault. I didn't think this through. I'm sorry. My mind isn't working on all four cylinders as of late."

I sent Milly a glare. "I can understand why both of you are feeling out of sorts, but Milly knows better. We've discussed—"

"Hush already," she said. "You two can talk somewhere besides the kitchen. And I promise not to eavesdrop. Can we go in? I'm sure Barkley needs to be let out, and I'm famished."

Rolling my eyes, I led them inside. "What are you making us, anyway?"

"Chicken stir-fry, if you drop the attitude."

"Fine. And thank you. Stir-fry sounds better than the egg sandwich I had in mind." Looking over at Richard, I noticed that he appeared to have lost ten pounds since we spoke last. "Are you still staying at the bed-and-breakfast?"

He placed an arm around Milly. "No. I've been staying at Milly's parents' place. They were all with me when I found this," he said, holding a piece of paper toward me.

Milly stepped forward. "You'll want a pair of gloves, Olive. My prints and Richard's are already on the note. We didn't know the darned thing was evidence until it was too late."

"Alright. Let me get my case. Milly, go ahead and let Barkley out. Richard, would you like to sit out there with Barkley while we talk?"

He sent a thoughtful smile. "Sounds good."

After retrieving my bag, I went straight to the kitchen to find Milly. "Do you have anything to say about what Richard received before I go out back, sly devil?"

Milly's stress had put her in a sour mood. "Seriously, Olive. Get off my back. As he said, me and my parents were with him when he found the stupid note, so I'm here to give him moral support. Is that okay with you? God, I'm cooking us dinner, for crying out loud."

My brow rose. "Um. Okay. I thanked you already, Milly. But I'm sorry. I know you're upset."

She scraped the cut-up chicken into the wok before turning toward me, her eyes glistening with tears. "I'm sorry too. It's not fair to take my stress out on you. And here all you're trying to do is solve this case. I'm such a brat."

I went around the counter and gave her a hug. "Yeah, you can be," I kidded. "But I promise to solve this case. Okay?"

Milly sniffled. "I know you will. Go on out. I'll have dinner ready shortly."

I pulled a bottle of Chardonnay from the fridge. "Get started without me," I said with a wink.

The corners of her mouth lifted. "No problemo."

Exiting my kitchen door, I joined Richard at the table on my deck.

He sent me a slight smile and threw the ball to Barkley. "Your dog is sweet. Maybe I should get one. I'm dreading the day when I go home to an empty house. But I'm gone so much that having a pet would make getting away complicated."

"Do you fly or drive?"

"I drive normally. I suppose the dog could accompany me most times."

I nodded. "Absolutely. I know lots of people who travel with their pets. Barkley and I have hit the road plenty of times. He's quite the road warrior, actually."

Barkley heard me talking about him and ran over to give me some love. "My dog has been a big blessing in my life, Richard. A pet would be good for you as well."

"Yeah, I just might take your advice." He placed the folded piece of paper on the table. "Before you read this, I want you to know that

I understand what we discuss stays between me, you, and Detective O'Malley. I will not talk about the case with Milly or anyone else."

I slipped a pair of gloves on and opened the paper, surprised to find the person had hand-written the contents.

It read,

Thorne,

My deed has done you a favor. I wrote this to say you are welcome. We all know Victoria deserved it. But show this to Harper or the police, and you will be next.

In place of a signature, they'd taped a tiny bundle of seeds to the paper.

I cringed inside, recalling Ethan's statement about the person possibly following me. And based on how the person addressed the parties by using last names, I felt this was the same person who'd typed the other note to me. The final touch of taping seeds drove the idea home in my mind.

"What do you think of this?" Richard asked in a shaky voice.

"Well, you shouldn't have brought this to my home, Richard. Based on the threat, you would have been safer to let Milly bring the note to the library."

His chin lifted. "She said the same thing, but I refuse to live in fear."

I wanted to say this didn't mean he needed to be careless, but at this point, I figured my opinion wouldn't change anything.

Richard's brow furrowed. "Why do you think the killer thinks they've done me a favor? What a preposterous thing to say to me."

I slipped the letter into an evidence bag. "Perhaps the perpetrator obtained some personal insight into your marriage."

"But Victoria and I were happy for the most part. No marriage is perfect."

I already knew the answer to my next question, but I'd not heard the explanation from Richard. Now I needed to.

I spoke in a gentle tone. "What made your marriage imperfect? Besides trivial stuff, of course. To your point, no marriage is perfect."

He sighed. "Do you know about the baby we lost? I wanted to have another child, but Victoria wouldn't hear of it. Many people know this, though, so it doesn't mean the killer was close to us."

I nodded. "I'm sure lots of people in Ballentine know about your loss. But what about here in Sparrow Haven?"

"No. I doubt many folks know around here."

"You would have already told me if you were suspicious about someone. Right?" I asked.

"Well, since we last talked, I've given a lot of thought about who could have done it. Ben Fields came to mind. He thought Victoria poisoned his dog. Did you know him and Marsha were our neighbors before they moved here?"

"Yes, I've questioned Ben, Marsha, and Linda."

"Who's Linda?"

"Ben had an affair with Linda after they moved here."

Richard chuckled. "That does not surprise me. Victoria and I heard them fighting from time to time. And when I say fighting, I don't mean just arguing."

"I get your drift. But some issues recently transpired. Based on the events, we don't believe Ben possessed knowledge about the method used to poison your wife. That's where we stand for now, anyway."

He nodded. "I see. Well, Ben is feisty, but I don't picture him the killing type."

"Has anyone else come to mind?"

"Not really. Like I told you before, Victoria hurt lots of people, and therefore, many resented her."

"Do you know Nancy Silverton or Chef Antonio? They helped Milly make the chowder."

He sighed. "Never heard of them."

"What about Cathy Mills or Monica Mills?"

He tapped his chin. "The names sound familiar, but I don't know why."

"Maybe because Victoria ruined Cathy's reputation as a chef, and the negative reviews ultimately shut Cathy's restaurant down. Do you recall anything about this?"

His eyes grew wide. "Yeah, I remember now. A reporter wrote an article about it. I read about the whole thing in the paper. I felt bad for the lady, but Victoria said the public needed to know."

"Did Victoria get food poisoning from eating at Cathy's restaurant?"

Richard batted the air. "Please. Victoria had a stomach made of steel. She was always exaggerating stuff and making up ridiculous lies."

"I see. Since you remember her now, do you know if Cathy and Victoria were ever friends?"

"No, I don't think so. They couldn't have been close friends anyway, or Victoria would have talked about her. I only know about Victoria's claims and about the restaurant closing."

Milly tapped on the kitchen window to let us know dinner was ready. I put a finger up, letting her know we'd be in shortly.

"Where did you find the note, Richard?"

"On the bottom porch step at Charles and Mary's house. Milly came over after work. We went on a walk, and then we found the note when we returned. The person set a rock on top. I guess to make sure the breeze didn't carry the paper off."

"Did you bring the rock with you?" I asked.

"No. I guess we were too shaken up to think of doing so."

"That's okay. I'll give Charles a call to ask him to find it. Did anyone stay at the house while you went walking?"

"No, all of us went."

"So, why did Milly arrive after you?"

"I told her I'd go alone and got an uber. But you know Milly."

I smiled. "Well, at least we can go enjoy some stir-fry now."

19

—·—

FOR THE LAST COUPLE of days, I'd wondered when Richard planned to have his wife's service. Having already uncovered the cause of death, he could have put Victoria to rest. But Richard told me that he thought burying her felt wrong, since he couldn't even begin having any closure until we caught her killer.

Aside from discussing the funeral, dinner with Richard and Milly turned out to be entertaining. They reminisced over memories they'd shared as families and discussed light topics about Victoria, such as her vivacious personality. Richard had a quirky sense of humor and made Milly and me laugh throughout our meal. I thought the time around the table had been good for all of us.

Milly stayed the night and let Richard take her car back to her parents' house since he hadn't had anything to drink.

The next morning, I awoke early, so I was in the kitchen making breakfast when Milly entered with Barkley, who loved waking her up. Milly sported a severe case of bedhead.

I cackled. "Tell me. Has Norman seen this side of you yet?"

Stretching, she yawned. "Please. He has seen way worse."

My brow rose. "Already, Milly? Really, it's a little soon...even for you," I kidded, gently flipping the frying eggs over.

Tossing a blueberry in her mouth, she sent me a playful glare. "I didn't know I was coming down for confession, Saint Olivia."

"Did you at least bring an open heart to receive my guidance and counsel?"

She sweetly smiled before sticking her tongue out. "You've seen the man, right? I'm only human. Anyway. How are you and Ethan doing? Set a date yet?"

I pulled the sizzling bacon from the oven. "Sure have...it's the same day you kiss a frog, and he turns into a prince."

She poured herself a cup of coffee and took a long inhale in. "Who needs a prince? All I need is Barkley's love and a good cup of coffee." She knelt to kiss Barkley and then took a sip of the brew. "Seems my dreams have all come true."

"Way to dream big," I said, laughing.

"Stop stalling and answer my question. Jeez. It's like pulling teeth with you this morning. I mean, you already have a prince if you hadn't noticed."

Full plates in hand, we took our seats. "Okay, okay. Yes, Ethan is charming, handsome, and...lots of good things. But we haven't had as much time together lately, and honestly, I've kind of liked the break."

"There's nothing wrong with time apart. Has he been making you feel guilty about the space?"

I bit off a piece of bacon, savoring the maple crunch. "No, on the contrary. He seems to respect my space."

"Hey... improvement! Ethan was putting the pressure on there for a while. I know how that can push you away from a guy."

I shrugged. "I know. But...it feels different lately."

She piled some egg on her fork before pointing the utensil toward me and sighing. "Get a ring on his finger already."

Rolling my eyes, I took a sip of coffee. "My bestie, who has no desire to marry...can't stop bringing the topic up to me? Why, pray tell?"

She did her cheesy grin. "Because I know what's best for you."

"Okay, Mom. Thank you, but I refuse to rush. I don't care if time isn't on my side."

She smacked her lips. "Yeah. No, it's really not," she said, winking. "Seriously though, I like to give you hell, but I agree. You are too old to rush into marriage, pop out a kid or two, and then get divorced. Not cool."

I kicked her foot under the table. "What do you really think about Norman? And I don't mean in bedhead situations."

She bit her lower lip in contemplation for several seconds. "I like him."

My mouth about fell to the floor. "Have I ever heard you say that?"

Milly batted at me. "Oh, stop it. You're gonna make me blush," she said, before laughing hysterically. "My luck with guys is truly that pathetic."

I covered my mouth against joining in. "No, this is good, Milly. What do you like about him?"

She shrugged. "I don't know. He's a big, muscular dork, and he makes me laugh."

I waved my hand. "Okay," I said, trying not to giggle. "Go on."

"What do you mean, go on? That's all. To be continued...I guess."

I smiled. "Fair enough. I'll take it."

"And I'll take this," she said, grabbing my bacon. "Like you said. I've got to go to work!"

"Oh, okay, says the owner. Ha-ha."

Watching Milly leave with a little hop in her step made my spirit lift. I'd missed Milly's smiles and laughter. There was light at the end of the tunnel, and I'd press on until the rays lit up the truth, and justice prevailed.

***

There was still an hour before the library opened, but I headed there in hopes of getting caught up on some back-office tasks. I hadn't taught Rose every task around the library, but she'd gone above and beyond in all the areas she'd received training. I would have been in a pickle otherwise.

Strolling down Main Street, the quaint charm of my small town always enveloped me in a comforting familiarity. The streets were dotted with locals going about their daily routines, and the air carried the gentle scent of blooming flowers from the storefronts lining the glistening sidewalk.

I was headed for my library, a place where I normally found the most complete solace. But as I walked up, I knew that today it was the setting for a rendezvous with the local news station. Fred had texted to let me know a reporter would be coming to interview me.

Approaching my library's entrance, I noticed a young reporter standing by, a notepad clutched in hand with a look of anticipation in her eyes. It was clear the murder case had stirred more than the usual curiosity in town.

The reporter shook my hand.

"Ms. Harper, my name is Blair Clarkson, and I'm from *Sparrow Haven Times*."

Despite my previous experiences with the paper, I'd not met this reporter before. "It's nice to meet you. Call me Olivia."

Her shoulders relaxed a notch. "Thanks for taking the time to talk with me. This is my first murder story, so I'm a bit nervous. But Detective O'Malley said you would be the one to interview."

I smiled, knowing exactly how their conversation had gone and how much Fred despised any type of limelight.

"You're welcome. Detective O'Malley told me you'd be dropping by. I always appreciate how your paper reports accurate and pertinent information for our community. Are you new to the area? Or just to S. H. Times?"

"I've been here six months. I worked as a reporter for a short time before moving here." She tapped her pen on her notepad. "Anyway, I promise not to take much of your time."

I invited her in, my heart heavy with the weight of the unsolved murder that had cast a shadow over our community. And I knew if the reporter printed an article, the paper would not provide the answers, which only time and more investigating could provide. While I wouldn't be able to speak about details, people needed to know we had the investigation well in hand, and we were striving for the truth with effectiveness and confidence.

I smiled and offered her a seat in front of the fireplace, trying to ease her air of awkwardness. "Ask away," I prompted.

"Can you start by telling me how you became involved in this case?"

"Sure. Over the years, I've helped Detective O'Malley solve crimes, and it's won me the Sparrow Haven sleuth award, you could say," I replied in a teasing tone. "In this particular case, I attended the tasting, and I was on the scene when Mrs. Thorne passed. Being a witness gave me some crucial insight into the crime. Detective O'Malley decided the best route was to ask me to be a consultant on the case."

"Is it true the killer used dried hemlock leaves to poison Mrs. Thorne?"

"Yes, they poisoned the clam chowder with hemlock. It's a very toxic species," I added, hoping she'd forget about what part of the plant the killer used.

It worked.

"How long did it take for...for," she stammered.

I ballparked the answer. "Less than ten minutes."

Blaire licked her lips. "Well, I'm glad she didn't...suffer long."

At this point, I figured I'd assist her in the interview since I didn't need to worry about her delving too deep.

I glanced down at her notepad. "You were about to ask me if the people who made the chowder have been arrested?"

She made a line through her next question. "Yes. Have they made any arrests thus far?"

"No, we questioned the cooks and found no cause to make any arrests at this time."

Blaire squared her shoulders. "Do you have any more suspects at this time?"

I'd expected her to inquire about Milly being my childhood best friend next. Seemed she hadn't done her homework well enough to know this relevant information.

"Yes, we have suspects we are looking into. But I can't comment further on who or why."

"What about Richard Thorne?"

A valid question, but poorly asked. This sweet reporter wasn't ready for the magnitude of this story, and I felt bad about her skill set not matching the intensity of the case. On the other hand, the situation couldn't be better for me. Usually, I had to really focus and tread lightly with the media.

"Yes, we questioned Mr. Thorne as well."

"Did he have an alibi?"

"I'm sorry. I have to respect Mr. Thorne's privacy, but I can tell you he has fully cooperated with this investigation and desires closure to this case."

I glanced at the clock then back at her.

"I know you need to open shortly. Just one more question, please?"

"Sure," I said, curiously, because they usually waited till the end to really try to stump me.

"I just love your shirt! Where did you get it?"

Glancing down, I stifled laughter. "At Style Haven. It is the third boutique on the right," I added, pointing toward the south end.

She stood and flipped her notepad shut. Her eyes held a light of expectation. "How did I do? I appreciate any feedback."

Clearing my throat, I pushed back a list of pointers. "Okay. So, a murder story is very complex. Just when you think you can't dig any deeper...dig some more."

I doubted Blaire's superior would assign her to another big story for a long time once she printed up a draft. But even in a small town, the media was a cut-throat business. For Blaire's sake, I hoped she developed a thick skin the way all writers have to.

20

I WAS SUPPOSED TO meet Fred at lunchtime to do what he called getting our ducks in a row. At this point, our suspect list was growing smaller, allowing us to zoom in on those remaining. And we needed to go over a to-do list to ensure we were leaving no loose ends in regard to the leads that had developed along the way.

After the reporter had left, I'd texted Fred and asked if we could meet at my mom's café. He'd texted back with, does a duck waddle? Apparently, my animal answers were rubbing off on him. Or, more likely, Fred either thought I'd find the response annoying the way he did, or I'd be annoyed at him stealing my thing.

Walking along the cobblestone path, I tucked my hands in my pockets, feeling the urge to clap with excitement. In some cases, breakthroughs happened shortly after this kind of meeting. Albeit sometimes we cleared the hurdles in weeks instead of days, but I'd take anything over the dead ends we'd run into thus far. Early on in this case, Fred had been quick to remind me that, on average, a murder case wasn't solved for months or even years. I'd not let him go any further than years and said I wouldn't accept either when Milly was involved.

The doorbell chimed merrily as I entered, announcing my arrival. The soft, rustic décor of my mom's café greeted my eyes with a charming mix of vintage paintings and weathered wooden furniture, and dappled sunlight streamed through the lace curtains.

At lunchtime, the café was a bustling hub of activity. The aroma of freshly brewed coffee, toasted bread, and savory spices wafted from the kitchen.

My mom's eyes lit up as she came out from behind the counter to hug me with a warm smile in an apron dusted with flour.

She laughed as I was in the habit of dusting my clothes off after an embrace at her café.

"Did I get any on you this time?" she asked, winking.

Glancing down, I shook my head. "I don't see a cloud today."

She made a pouty face. "Well, that must mean I didn't hug you good enough." She hugged me again before glancing at the far corner of the room. "Mr. Ornery Pants is over there," she said, titling her head.

I smiled. "What do you gauge the meter at this morning?"

"It's at about forty percent on the ornery meter."

"Oh good. I'm in luck."

"Come to the house for dinner this evening. We've missed you."

"Wish I could, but I can't. Ethan has something planned for this evening."

My mom clasped her hands together. "How lovely. Tell him we said hello."

"I will," I said, giving her a hug. "I know you're busy. And Fred doesn't like to be kept waiting."

She winked. "This is true. The meter might go up if you keep dilly-dallying."

Sure enough, Fred stood and shrugged as if to say, what the heck?

Going over to our table, I firmly set my purse down and took my notes out. "Seriously, Detective Cranky? I can't say hello to own mother?"

"Of course, you can. I gave you a few minutes, didn't I?"

"Gee, thanks. You are boundlessly gracious."

"Well?" he asked. "How did you like the animal-based answer? Annoying, right?"

I laughed. "Aw, not at all. I must be rubbing off on you. Your response made me picture a cute, little duck waddling. So, keep 'em coming."

He grunted. "Must not have the same effect in text, be my guess."

"What did you order for lunch today?"

"Can we cut the small talk? I've got a busy afternoon."

Maybe he was at forty percent with my mom. I'd gauge the meter with me to be at about eighty percent.

I drummed my fingers on the table. "Sure. Let's start with how you told Blair Clarkston to interview me at my library."

He shrugged. "Would you have preferred your home?"

"No, but a thank you right here at this table would be nice."

"I figured you'd be good at that stuff."

"I'll take it. You're welcome." I glanced around the room. "How long ago did you order?"

"I told your mom we'd both get our orders to go."

I shrugged. "Fine with me. We need to be totally focused."

He winked. "That's right, kiddo."

"Oh, good, the meter is falling now."

"Huh?"

"Never mind. So, where do you want to start?"

He slid his phone towards me, a list displayed on the screen. "Does our suspect list match?"

I scanned his phone. "Yep."

"Alright. So, the two clam chowder cooks. Start there."

"Um, okay. Well, Nancy Silverton. She lied to her son, saying we had the killer in custody. Since Seth thought we had a closed case, he withheld nothing from me. Nancy told us she had no hard feelings toward Victoria, but Seth said his mom hated her ever since the harsh critique almost ruined her livelihood."

"Okay, so Nancy either lied for fear of looking guilty, or she's hiding something. Thoughts on her son?"

"Seems to me Seth's likely innocent. From the way he spilled the beans, he truly believed his mom's story. Seth's purpose in speaking to me was to thank me for catching the killer and clearing Nancy's name."

Fred's eyes narrowed. "Or his claim was an act. What a creative way to take the spotlight off of him."

"But to share the bit about his mom hating Victoria 'til the end? Kind of thoughtless."

"Maybe Seth has a grudge against his mom. Maybe he knew the killer hadn't been caught, and he made the story up about his mom to put her in the hot seat."

"Well, if so, he lied about their relationship. Seth said he and his mom had looked after one another his whole life. His dad's never been in the picture."

Fred crossed his arms. "That being the case, his story is more believable. Single moms who raise a son on their own usually form a loyal bond. These sons are typically big-time mama's boys."

"Am I hearing a but?"

"Yeah. Can't put my finger on what it is," he answered, jotting something down. "Let's move on for now."

"All I have written about Antonio is his comment to Larry about how they'd made some killer clam chowder."

Fred shrugged. "I doubt Antonio would have said that if he planned to poison the chowder, but I'll note the comment."

"If Antonio cared about Victoria, he sure isn't showing any interest in our investigation."

"Maybe the man is just glad we are leaving him alone? Sure, Antonio had a crush on Victoria. If I'd gotten wind that the crush was actually an obsession, I'd be more suspicious. Either way, if I were a suspect in a murder investigation, I'm sure I'd be staying below the surface, too," Fred added.

"Alright," I said. "That leaves Cathy Mills and her daughter, Monica."

Fred nodded. "Both definitely have motive."

My brow rose. "But you said Monica's alibi checked out, and we know Cathy is deathly ill."

"That's right."

"By the way, I asked Richard Thorne if he knew Cathy Mills. At first, he wasn't sure. But after I told him about Victoria shutting down her tavern, Richard said he remembered reading about the incident in the paper. I'm not sure this bit is important, but I wanted you to know he verified the story."

Fred titled his head. "About Cathy being ill...did you know I talked to Ethan about stage two lung cancer?"

My brow furrowed. "No. What did Ethan say?"

"Are you two not talking much lately? Your boy is always a good bit of help on cases."

"Sure, we talk. I've just been..."

"Self-absorbed?"

I scowled. "Are you kidding me, Fred? You know where I've been emotionally since this whole thing happened."

"Ah. In your shell?"

"That's one way to describe my present state."

Fred leaned in. "Well, get out of the darned thing. You need his help."

I huffed. "I've done a good job in the past without Ethan."

"And you've done even better with him. Look, in solving crime, you know you have to leave feelings out of it. When you're working a case with Ethan, he's your sleuth partner. Period."

"Jeez. Fine. Well, what did Ethan tell you about stage two lung cancer?"

"He said individuals in stage two can have days when they feel okay, with few symptoms, giving them less discomfort. How taxing is the act of poisoning chowder? All they did was pour some powder in the mix."

"Okay, but then the person planted evidence in a storage unit." I shook my head. "I guess they could have done so the same day after you had finished your search."

I then told Fred about the note Richard Thorne and Milly found on her parents' doorstep. "Our killer is moving about in an active manner. And they are energetically toying with us."

"All good points. But not the one I'm trying to make here."

I pinched the bridge of my nose. "Alright. I should have thought to ask Ethan about stage two lung cancer myself. Or at least researched it."

"Right. And when did you plan on telling me about the threat Richard received?"

My mood was quickly dropping to meet his. "Fred. Richard found the note yesterday. I received the evidence literally last night. And I brought the note with me today."

He glanced down at the floor. "I don't see your case."

"I sealed the note up, and I have it in my purse. What's up with you today?"

Fred reached across the table and patted my hand. "I'm sorry, kiddo. This freakin' murderer is messing with all our heads. But we have a lot going for us, and it's largely because of you. Will you forgive an old, grumpy detective?"

I grinned. "Does a snake hiss?"

"I'll ignore that. But you bring up something else we need to figure out."

"The copperhead."

"Yes," he stated. "And you're right about another thing, too. Our killer is active indeed. The culprit may pay attention to details, but their games are cocky to a fault. Let's hope they keep up the shenanigans."

Just then, my mom brought over our to-go bags. "Two tuna and avocado wraps."

Fred pulled his out and unwrapped it. "I can't wait another minute. I'm hungry."

I laughed. "Oh my gosh. You're eating healthy?"

"I do from time to time." Chewing, he glanced at my mom. "Let's keep what else is in the bag between us."

Taking a seat next to me, she zipped her lips. "Do you have time to visit for a few, dear?"

"Sure, Mom," I answered, emptying my bag. "I guess I'll eat too. The wrap looks divine."

Fred looked surprised as he studied the wrap in his hand. "I can see why you get this so often, kiddo."

"Mom, did you remember the rock?"

"I did. And your dad followed your instructions on how to bag the evidence."

"What rock?" Fred asked.

"The culprit placed the rock on the note," Mom interjected. "You know, to serve as a paper weight."

Fred shook his head. "How many things is this idiot going to touch and hand over?"

My mom leaned in. "You think they might turn themselves in? Or do they just want to be caught?"

"No and no," Fred answered. "But they're leaving breadcrumbs. I find the fact odd."

"You said they're just boasting," I said.

"And I still believe they are. Maybe there is something more to the clues than we're seeing."

"Connect the dots," I whispered. "Maybe solving this case is about connecting the dots."

Fred smirked. "I've always liked those kinds of puzzles."

"But the game is so easy," Mom said.

"No, not always," Fred stated. "I've worked some complicated games. They can make your eyes cross," he said while crossing his eyes.

My mom laughed. "Uncross your eyes, Fred. You could lose your reputation with that silly expression." She put her arm around me. "You must have brought the meter way down, dear. Well done."

Fred inhaled his last few bites and stood. "I need to go. Thanks for lunch, Margaret."

"What about a to-do list?"

"Let's both come up with our own and keep each other posted."

He took the evidence from my mom, grabbed his lunch bag, and waved.

I called after him. "You have a strawberry cheesecake Danish in the bag. Am I right?"

"Close," he said, still walking off.

Mom laughed. "You're basically right on, Olivia. He ordered a cherry cheesecake Danish."

21

THAT EVENING, ETHAN SURPRISED me with a spontaneous adventure, and as we made our way to the docks for a whale-watching excursion, my heart brimmed with excitement. The evening sun bathed the seaside town in a soft, golden glow, and a crisp, salty breeze carried the promise of an unforgettable experience.

The bustling harbor welcomed us with the rhythmic symphony of seagulls overhead, their calls blending with the cheerful chatter of fellow passengers awaiting the same adventure. The scent of briny sea air, a delightful mixture of saltwater and seaweed, wrapped around me like a comforting embrace.

As we approached the sturdy vessel that would take us into the open waters, I felt the rough, weathered texture of the wooden handrail beneath my fingers. The boat bobbed gently against the dock, and I could sense the power of the ocean beneath us, like a slumbering giant waiting to reveal its secrets.

Once aboard, we found a prime spot on the upper deck, where the unobstructed view of the horizon stretched out before us. The soft hum of the boat's engine rumbled as we set sail, and the constant rocking motion soothed my senses.

Ethan stood beside me, a warm smile on his handsome face as he pointed out into the expanse. "I can't imagine anything more spectacular."

I got on my tiptoes and kissed his cheek. "You won't have to imagine if we get lucky enough to see the main reason for this excursion."

"How many times have you gone whale watching?"

"I've lost count, but this excursion never gets old. The experience is brand new each and every time. Thanks for planning this. Your timing is impeccable."

He put his arm around my waist and drew me closer. "I figured you could use a distraction. You been doing okay?"

I bit my lower lip. "I'm sorry. I can be like a turtle sometimes, going into my shell to process things. And the hiding away is nothing new, so my habit has nothing to do with you. Or us."

"I wasn't worried that going into your shell was about me or us. But I liked hearing the words all the same."

I laughed. "You are so transparent. Milly explained all of this to you, right?"

He grinned. "I won't lie. She did. But I didn't go to her this time. Milly reached out to me. Speaking of Milly...Norman is falling head over heels for her."

"She tends to have that effect on men. Milly told me she likes Norman, and that's big. It's been ages since she's said that about a guy."

"I hope it works out for them. They both deserve happiness."

Despite our casual banter, as I gazed out at the vast expanse of the Atlantic Ocean, the anticipation in the air was electric.

The sea had transformed into a brilliant shade of cerulean, its surface rippling like a quilt of liquid diamonds under the sun. The cadence of waves, each one rising and falling in harmony, had a mesmerizing effect, lulling me into a state of tranquil expectancy.

Then, the main event happened. A collective gasp from passengers drew my attention to a majestic sight. Emerging from the depths of the ocean, a colossal creature breached the surface, its sheer size and power leaving me in blissful wonder. Our gift was a humpback whale, a gentle giant of these waters.

The whale's massive body arched gracefully, suspended in mid-air for a moment, as if it were offering a graceful bow to the world above. The mammal's grey skin glistened in the sunlight and shimmered like stardust against the deep blue backdrop.

As the humpback descended back into the water, it left behind a mesmerizing spectacle. The surrounding waves cascaded and frothed, creating a temporary ballet of liquid splendor. The intense sound of the ocean, momentarily disrupted by the whale's powerful emergence, settled into a soothing serenade once more.

The humpback's immense fluke rose briefly above the surface before it created a grand splash as the tail submerged back into the depths.

Ethan's smile reached his eyes. "That was epic!"

My hand went to my heart. "Every time."

"Do you think we'll see anything else?"

I pointed out in the distance, along the rugged coastline, where I'd spotted a colony of seals lounging on sun-kissed rocks. Their dark, round eyes regarded us with a sense of curiosity, but they seemed content to continue their sunbathing. The seals stretched, yawned contently, and occasionally splashed into the water for a playful swim.

"Now, that's the life," Ethan said, chuckling.

"I know, right?"

We sailed in serene silence for a while, Ethan's hand massaging the back of my neck.

"You're going to put me to sleep if you keep that up. Your hand feels so good," I said, turning toward him.

I glanced around to see we were alone in our spot of the boat, and the people speckling the vicinity were focused on the wonderous sights before them.

Ethan must have seen the emotions swarming my face as I looked into his eyes. He cupped my face, his eyes filling with an intensity that mirrored my own feeling. Our faces drew together, and the world seemed to hold its breath. Our lips met in a tender, lingering kiss. And in that moment, the ocean, the waves, and the universe itself bore witness to the profound connection we shared.

As we finally pulled away, our foreheads touched in quiet acknowledgment. He whispered my name, his breath tickling my face.

I cleared my throat and turned to face the railing. "Look," I said, to change the subject.

Above us, the sky was alive with the graceful flight of seabirds. Gulls, terns, and shearwaters soared on the ocean breeze, their wings catching the golden hues of the setting sun. Occasionally, one would swoop low, skimming the water's surface in search of a meal and then ascend again with effortless grace.

I looked back at Ethan to find him staring at me.

Despite a slight hurt lurking in the dark depths of his eyes, his mouth curved up in the corners. "You're so beautiful. I don't tell you enough."

I put my hand on his chest. "You are always generous with your compliments, Ethan. And they mean a lot. So, thank you." I winked. "Did you know you are drop-dead gorgeous?"

He chuckled. "You seem to be alive and well."

I smiled. "I see women stare at you all the time. I'd get mad, but I can't blame them."

He shook his head. "Really? I've never noticed."

"Such a terrible liar."

"Want to go inside for a bit?"

The air had taken on a slightly cooler edge, and the sun, now a fiery orb on the horizon, appeared much larger than on land.

With fingers intertwined, we ventured inside the cabin of the boat. The dimmed interior was bathed in the soft glow of overhead lights, contrasting with the fading daylight outside. The faint scent of the sea lingered in the air.

The cabin boasted rows of cushioned seats that faced large panoramic windows. A sense of camaraderie filled the room as passengers found their spots, their hushed conversations punctuated by excited whispers about the sightings we had witnessed.

We settled into a pair of plush seats by the window, our shoulders touching as we watched the ocean's changing colors through the glass. The boat rocked with the rhythm of the waves, creating a lullaby-like sensation, adding to the cabin's cozy atmosphere. In this tranquil moment, the vicinity cocooned us in our own world, where the ocean danced just beyond the windowpane.

"I want to ask you a question, and please don't freak out."

I felt the air leave my lungs, hoping Ethan wasn't about to ruin a perfect evening.

Not trusting my voice, I nodded.

He tucked strands of hair behind my ear. "Are you like Milly when it comes to marriage?"

My brow creased. "No. I'm not opposed to marriage. Not at all."

He nodded. "Okay. What about kids?"

I fidgeted with the button on my cardigan. "If the timing is right, I'm not opposed to having one. Maybe two, but I'm not sure." I held my breath before continuing. "I know you want kids. Unless your mind has changed since your first marriage?"

"I have this empty spot in my heart. I have a feeling only a child can fill the hole."

My eyes grew wide at his deep description. I didn't know how to respond, so I stayed silent.

"Do you have an empty feeling somewhere inside, or am I the only one?"

Turning toward him, I took his hand and held it with both of mine. "Ethan, I think it would be amazing to have a child someday. But I don't ache for one like you're describing."

He smiled, but the expression lacked joy. "I'm glad you don't. This feeling is no fun."

Then an idea struck me like a lightning bolt. Was Ethan trying to guilt me into rushing into marriage? I certainly hoped not because that would be disturbing.

"Well, I hope your empty spot in your heart gets filled one day."

He made a sour face. "What is that supposed to mean?"

I really didn't want to argue again. "Nothing bad. I'm just saying I hope you have a child someday...like you want."

His eyes narrowed. "I heard a bit of sarcasm in your voice when you said it the first time."

I sighed. "Look, you wanted to talk about the subject, and we did. Let's leave the conversation at that, please."

His voice was low and stressed. "I appreciate you talking to me about marriage and kids, but we are not done."

"How are we not done? You asked me. I answered and vice versa."

"No, because we should feel closer after talking about something so personal. And I'm not feeling close like we were before."

I kept my voice calm despite my blood pressure rising. "Ethan, please understand. I'm in the middle of the most troublesome case I've ever tried to solve. And it's a murder investigation involving my best friend. Do I really have to spell this out to you? I don't need any added stress."

His hand flew to his forehead. "I'm pushing you again. And at the worst time. I'm sorry. And I do appreciate you talking with me about marriage and kids. Thinking back, you opened up, and that means the world to me. So, thank you. I'm a stupid guy sometimes."

I squeezed his hand. "You're allowed to be imperfect. The fact makes me feel more normal," I added, smirking. And then I changed the subject to a safer subject. "How are your parents? You haven't mentioned them in a while."

"They're enjoying retirement, doing some traveling. You might get to meet them. They'd like to visit soon and see my home, and they're excited about meeting you."

"I look forward to meeting them as well. What are they like?"

"My dad is a retired Marine."

"Yeah, I remember."

"Right. So, he's ornery and blunt. You never have to worry about where you stand with him. My mom is an angel. You'll love her." He leaned in and kissed me. "I've really enjoyed our evening."

I kissed him back. "Me too."

22

— • —

"WOULD YOU LIKE TO come in for a nightcap, Ethan?" I asked as he turned into my driveway.

He winked. "What kind of nightcap?"

"Ha-ha. Actually, I thought we could go over my case notes. But only if—"

"Yes. Yes. Yes. I've been curious about those notes of yours."

I smiled. "Good. And make sure you tell Fred we did so the next time you talk to him."

"Why?"

"He scolded me this morning for working this case by myself for the most part."

"I don't see it that way. We've talked about the case several times. And we met at the fair to search the tasting grounds."

Getting out of the car, I put my hands on my hips. "I totally should have told Fred what you just said."

Ethan chuckled. "I think Fred enjoys giving you a hard time. It's his quirky way of showing he cares, is all."

"Sounds like Fred all right," I said before breathing in the crisp night air.

The summer evening had draped a tapestry of twilight hue over my home. Fireflies flickered like tiny stars in the darkness. Ethan and I stepped inside, greeted by the comforting scent of home.

Barkley had sensed our return, and his excitement was palpable as he wagged his tail furiously and emitted a single bark to welcome us.

"Let's take you outside," I said to Barkley, patting him.

The motion of the backdoor turned on the deck lights along the back of my home. The warm, earthy scent of summer flora mingled with the hint of freshly cut grass as we stepped outside. Barkley bounded down the deck steps and into the yard. An array of string lights overhead cast a soft amber illumination around his playful movements.

Through the tree branches, the full moon emerged like a radiant pearl in the night sky.

"We couldn't have asked for better weather this evening," Ethan said with a contented sigh.

I smiled, thinking about our perfect evening. "Agreed."

Allowing Barkley some time to explore around the backyard, Ethan pulled me onto his lap and breathed me in.

I draped my arm around his neck. "Have you received Barkley's blood work yet?"

"Yes. Today, actually. I should have told you earlier. We received a good report."

A weight lifted the way it always did when receiving good news about Barkley because of the heart disease he'd been diagnosed with as a puppy.

"Do you think Barkley will ever need surgery?"

"Of course I want to tell you no, but there's really no way of knowing. With the good care and love he receives, though, I'm optimistic he'll live a long, healthy life, Olivia."

I got up and opened the back door. Barkley took the hint and bounded towards the house.

"Can I interest you in a Dark 'n' Stormy? It's a cocktail with dark rum and ginger beer."

"I never say no to rum."

I made our beverages and then we went to sit in my den. Pulling out my notepad, I flipped through the pages to the notes taken during my meeting with Fred this morning, and I read them aloud.

"Sounds like you and Fred focused on the suspects, mostly."

"Yeah, I guess we did."

He rubbed his jawline. "Then let's focus on all the evidence we've acquired."

"Good idea."

"So, the note to Richard Thorne. What kind of paper did the culprit use?"

"Nothing special," I stated. "White copy paper."

Ethan shrugged. "And they wrote to you on a sticky note. Nothing unique there. The note to Richard. What do you make of the content?" he asked.

"I think the killer was being sarcastic."

"In other words, the killer doesn't think Richard views his wife's murder as a favor?"

"No. I think from their twisted perspective, the killer thinks they did the community a favor. Not Richard in particular."

"How sure are you?"

I flipped back a few pages. "I'm pretty sure. The last part of the note reads: 'We all know Victoria deserved it. The killer is justifying their murder by claiming everyone felt she deserved to die.' And then, the first part of the note reads: 'My deed has done you a favor. I wrote this to say you're welcome. The last part sounds sarcastic.'"

Ethan nodded. "I see your point. When someone says you're welcome without receiving a thank you first, they're usually being sarcastic."

"Exactly. And their note to me reads: Catch me if you can, Harper."

Ethan took a sip of his cocktail. "Again, they sound sarcastic."

"Exactly. And in both notes, the writer addresses us by our last names. This is no coincidence. The killer wrote both notes."

"What did the handwriting look like on Richard's note?"

I pulled up the photo of the note on my phone and handed my device to Ethan.

He studied the writing. "They used a mixture of caps and lowercase letters in each word. Each letter varies in size. And every word is angled differently."

"Yeah, obviously, to make the writing untraceable. But why handwrite it at all? Fred thinks they did so for the same reason they handed over the mortar and pestle."

"Boasting their confidence of never being caught?" he asked.

I nodded. "Right, but why take the risk and hand over all this evidence?"

"Maybe the killer isn't the one planting all of the evidence," Ethan said. "Maybe it's someone else giving us the evidence. And perhaps the culprit doesn't even know they are helping us solve the case."

I tapped my chin. "Interesting thought. Okay, so the note to Richard and the note to me match. And the weapon they delivered to me on a silver platter...It all seems to fit together. But the copperhead snake? I don't think the person who wrote the notes and planted the weapon brought a snake to the library. The copperhead gives off a totally different vibe."

"Good point. A killer who used poison to kill Victoria delivers a venomous snake to you—clearly a threat."

"Right. That part makes sense."

"So, I have two questions. Who gained access to the storage unit? Because there was no sign of forced entry. And who had access to a copperhead snake? Because that breed is not native to New England."

I took a sip of my drink, enjoying the warmth of the rum against the sweetness of the ginger. "Fred says the person either obtained it from Herb's aquarium, or they likely got it illegally without the proper permits. Based on Fred's team investigating Herb's employees and camera footage, the latter is the case."

Ethan glanced at his watch. "Sounds to me like we need to focus on the place where the murder happened, then."

Yawning, I stood. "I know you have an early morning, Ethan. Thanks for an amazing night. And thanks for your help on the case, too."

Downing his last sip, he stood and kissed me. "You're welcome. I have a feeling that if I'm right, and someone is ratting on the killer...if we find out who planted the evidence, they'll lead us to the murderer."

"You mean like, they'll tell us who killed Victoria?"

"Not directly. But I think they'll guide our steps to the culprit."

"Funny you say that. Fred said he had a feeling the evidence seemed to serve as a "connect the dots" kind of game. But he didn't understand why the perpetrator would leave a trail. I think you're right, Ethan...It is someone who is close to the killer."

***

The next morning, I arrived at the library early again to find a treasure in the donation box. Someone had donated what appeared to be a historic manuscript. Upon further assessment, the story was a precious relic of a bygone era. The delicate pages, yellowed with time and bearing the faint scent of history, awaited my careful attention. Having a dad who was a historian, I'd learned the art of preservation well. I smiled, picturing this unique addition framed and hanging on the library wall next to the historic area.

Seated cross-legged on the plush rug, I was quickly immersed in a task that required both patience and a keen eye.

With a white cotton glove adorning my hand, I began the delicate process of gently turning the pages. Each rustle of paper held a symphony of whispers as if sharing secrets of the past.

I reached for a soft brush with fine bristles, and with meticulous care, I swept away the dust and debris that had settled between the pages. I guided the brush along the edges, coaxing the hidden details to reveal themselves. Next, I repaired the weak areas with archival tape, a transparent lifeline to support the paper without compromising its historical integrity. And over the next hour, I felt like a guardian of the past, preserving the whispers of history for future generations to enjoy.

Checking the grandfather clock, I had fifteen minutes before opening. After transferring my project to the back room, I made a fresh pot of coffee and opened the box of scones I'd picked up from Vivi's café. I couldn't afford to provide breakfast treats every day, but once a month didn't break the bank.

I'd assisted a handful of members before I glanced across the library to see a woman with smooth, milk-chocolate colored skin and shiny, black hair she'd pulled back into a soft bun at the nape of her neck. I recognized her from the tasting.

"May I help you?" I asked.

She answered me with a lovely accent. "I would like to check out this book," she answered, holding up a book about herbal remedies.

"Of course. Would you like to get a library card, so you can check the book out?"

She nervously laughed. "Oh. I guess so. In school, I didn't need a card."

I smiled. "A public library is different, but I won't need any personal information. Just your name, and an email address so I can assign you a card. Then you can check out up seven books at a time, and I'll give you a slip with the return date."

Her dark-almond eyes lit up. "I remember in school that the librarian did the same. But I just want this one book for today." She shook my hand. "My name is Nina Gomez."

This was Antonio's wife. "I'm Olivia Harper. You're Antonio's wife?" I asked, leading her to my desk.

She opened the cover and nodded. "I am. I saw you at the tasting. You are Milly's friend, yes?"

"That's right. How is Antonio doing? He knew Victoria for several years, right?"

She took her thumb and made the pages in the book flip rapidly from beginning to end. "For years, yes. Antonio was very fond of Mrs. Thorne. He respected her culinary expertise. But my husband is like most men. He doesn't want to talk about his feelings, but I know he's upset."

"How so?"

She tucked the book under her arm as her eyes shifted down. "Instead of acting sad, he's mad all the time. At me," she added with more nervous laughter. "I'm used to his ways, though. We've been married for twenty-three years."

"Men tend to lash out at whoever they love most, don't they?"

"I know you help Detective O'Malley solve crimes. I hope you find the bad man soon."

"You think we are looking for a man?"

She covered her mouth. "No. Sorry, I didn't mean...I meant man or woman."

"I've heard Victoria could be harsh toward chefs. Did Antonio ever get offended or hurt by her?"

"I haven't been around them much. The times I have, she was either warm or cold towards him. I think she may have been the moody sort. Antonio sometimes joked about Mrs. Thorne to me. He called her two-faced."

I figured I knew what this meant, but I wanted to hear as much from Nina. "What did Antonio mean by two-faced?"

"One time, she would be all smiles and warm, but the next time she'd be all pouty and cold. He never knew what face to expect."

"I hope Antonio didn't take the different moods personally. She tended to be warm or cold toward everyone."

"My husband takes everything personally. Especially if it is someone he has on a pedestal," she added, giggling.

I handed her a card. "Are you looking for a particular remedy, Nina?"

This time, her laughter was light. "Yes, for the heartburn my husband is causing me."

23

—·—

As I approached the last stretch leading to the fairgrounds' office, the sky began to reveal its New England, capricious nature. Dark clouds gathered ominously overhead, and a low rumble of thunder echoed in the distance. It appeared nature had decided to add an unexpected twist to the last part of my journey.

The first drops descended lightly, their gentle pitter-patter offering a subtle warning. Within fifteen minutes, I watched the ground in front of my feet as droplets splattered on the dirt path, creating delicate ripples on the small puddles that had formed.

Soon, nature's intentions became clear. The drizzle intensified into a deluge as the wind picked up. At this point, I had a choice to make. I could allow the unexpected weather to sour my mood, or I could embrace the unexpected change and enjoy my outing under the darkening sky. So, I chose to appreciate the soothing dance of the wind-tossed leaves surrounding me and the fragrant scent of wet foliage.

Despite my adventurous spirit, when I arrived at the office, its weathered façade offered a welcome respite from the unexpected elements. Pushing open the door, I stepped inside, the dry air welcoming me. My clothes were drenched, and a pool of rainwater collected on the stone floor around my feet. Thank heavens I'd worn dark colors today.

Just then, Larry came around the corner. "Forgot your umbrella, Olivia?" He retrieved a towel from the break room and handed it to me. "I'm kidding, of course. Came out of nowhere," he added, chuckling. "You look like a drowned rat. A pretty one, though."

I smiled. "I've never met a pretty rat. But thank you."

"I still can't believe what you found at the storage unit the other day."

"I'm still wrapping my head around the finding as well."

He crossed his hairy arms. "What brings you back here? Hoping to find more evidence on a silver platter?"

"Wouldn't mind if I did. But no. Would you mind showing me the key peg where all the storage unit keys are kept?"

Larry took me to the manager's lounge and pointed to the far wall. The peg accounted for all five keys.

"Are you the only one in the office today?" I asked.

"For now. We're all in and out of here during events."

"I see. Well, I'm glad I caught you."

"I'll say. But you may need a boat to get back if this storm keeps up."

I laughed. "You know how the weather is around here. I'm sure a blue sky will emerge shortly."

Larry pulled out a chair for me before taking a seat. "You came back here hoping to find answers, though, right?"

I shrugged. "Something like that."

He pulled a Tootsie Roll from his shirt pocket and then offered me one.

"No, thanks."

Unwrapping it, he popped the candy into his mouth. "You know, it's too bad the killer typed the note. My uncle is a retired writing analyst. He taught me a thing or two about how he deciphered handwriting."

"Really?" I asked, getting my phone out. "I do have a handwritten note."

I gave him my phone after pulling up the picture of the note, figuring we could use all the help we could get. Fred hadn't heard back from our forensic document examiner yet.

Larry stared at the display and grunted. "We got a trickster on our hands. They were smart to mix up the writing in so many ways."

"Would you mind sending the pic to your uncle?"

Larry snorted. "Would you believe the poor fella lost his vision? Uncle Tony is about blind as a bat from macular degeneration and glaucoma. Ironic, right? Since he used to use his eyes to make a living."

I frowned. "How terrible. I'm sorry."

Larry batted the air, still studying the pic. He put the phone on the table and hunched over it with intensity. Using his fingers, Larry blew up the pic and examined each part of the note.

Just when I thought Larry was going to hand my phone back with nothing to say, he cleared his throat in a business type manner.

He spoke low and slow, all the while keeping his eyes glued to my phone. "The curvature of these letters and the deliberate slants suggests a certain confidence but not extravagance. And precision perhaps."

My brow rose in surprise. "Okay. Anything else?"

He picked up my phone and leaned back as he studied some more. "Despite all the sporadic letters, I think there is a sense of flow to the writing. It's not rushed, and they have a steady hand."

I whipped out my notebook at this point to write down all he'd said so far. "I'm impressed. Can you decipher an age or gender?"

Larry's face beamed with pride. "My guess is that the writer is of a mature age because a few of the letters, although they are not connected, appear cursive-like. And I'm fairly certain a woman wrote this."

"Why?"

"My uncle says women typically use more rounded and flowing strokes, while men's handwriting is usually more angular and blocky. And the letters are on the small side. On average, women write smaller letters. Last, two lower case letters have slight loops." Pointing, he showed me an example. "I hope I'm right, but I could be rusty."

"Either way, thank you."

"No. Thank you. I can't believe I'm helping solve a murder! And it brings back lots of good memories. Examining handwriting became like a game in my family. We were quite competitive too," he added, chuckling.

"I can see how this activity could be a fun game."

Larry stood and went to the fridge. "I'm going to have a bite to eat." He pulled out a whole pizza. "Want a piece? Or something to drink?"

"I'm fine but thank you. Actually, do you have a computer I could use?"

"It runs slower than a snail, but sure. And if you need access to any HR files, let me know."

"You have access to HR files?"

He tore a piece of pizza from the pie and nodded. "You wouldn't think it to look at me, but I'm the HR guy. Everything else I do around here is purely on a volunteer basis. I get bored easily."

I tapped my pen on my notebook, watching him devour the slice. "You do all the hiring?"

Larry tossed the crust and dove in for another piece. "Sure. I hire ride operators, ticket sellers, food vendors, and security personnel.

But my favorite part of this job is dealing with issues and mediating conflict. This place can be one big soap opera."

"I guess you know Ben Fields, then?"

"Ah, the lemonade man. Generous dude. He supplied free lemonade for all the tasting competitors."

"I don't recall seeing Ben at the tasting. And his stand is next to the Ferris wheel, right?"

"Ben was working his stand during the tasting. And yes, he typically sets up by the big wheel. He brought several gallons of lemonade by earlier that morning. We stored them in the storage unit fridge."

"Did you unlock the building for him?"

"Nah. I gave him the key, but he brought it back to me after the short-lived tasting. No pun intended." He tossed another crust and picked up another piece in one motion. "I'm sorry. I didn't mean to make light of the matter. Victoria was a dear friend of mine."

"Did Ben ever talk about Victoria?"

Larry talked and chewed at the same time. "Everyone who knows Ben knows he despised Victoria because of some falling out they had back when they were neighbors."

This new information caused my head to spin, and I suddenly needed to be alone. Fred and I had all but ruled out Ben Fields, but now I'd learned Ben, along with his motive, was present at the tasting site the morning of the murder and, even more, that he had the storage unit key in his possession. Fred would say I'd obtained enough circumstantial evidence for law enforcement to make an arrest.

"Is there a place where I can make a call privately, please?"

Picking up another piece of pizza, Larry motioned for me to follow. "Take as much time as you need, Olivia."

I waited for Larry to exit the office before plopping down at the desk. Putting my elbows on the wooden surface, I buried my face in my hands and shook my head. I needed to talk to Ethan, so I sent him a text. He called me seconds later.

"Hey, beautiful."

I went and shut the office door. "Hey. Sorry to bother you at work."

"You are never a bother, darling. Everything all right?"

I brought him up to speed on everything Larry and I discussed. Silence followed.

"I don't know where to start. Larry evaluates handwriting? And he's in HR? I apparently judge books by their covers."

"That's where you start? I needed to talk about Ben Fields. Not Hairy Larry."

"I know," he said, chuckling. "You sound frustrated. I only meant to lighten your mood."

"I'm confused. Let's say Ben is our killer. Why the shenanigans at the police station? His actions don't match up with someone guilty of murder. What am I missing?"

"Maybe the whole fiasco about the dried hemlock leaves and the display at the station are doing exactly what Ben intended. He's got you and Fred close to striking him off the suspect list."

"If Ben is the killer, who is planting the clues?"

"Maybe I was wrong. Maybe Ben is doing all of it. He's got you in a state of frustration. I'd say if Ben killed Victoria, he's covering his trail well."

"Then why is my gut screaming that he isn't our preparator?"

"A gut can be wrong."

I thought back to almost marrying the wrong man. Until I'd caught him cheating, I felt in my gut we were right for each other. "I suppose, since I almost married a cheater."

Ethan chuckled. "No. That one is about your heart. And a heart can fool even the wisest of people."

I groaned. "See? My head is spinning. I can't make sense of anything."

"You need to give yourself some credit. Every time we talk, you have new information to share. Just take a breather and then get back to doing what you're doing. With your talent, a breakthrough is about to happen. I know it."

"Does your gut know it? Or your heart?"

He laughed. "Both."

"I'm so uncomfortable. The rain drenched me from head to toe on the way here."

"That's the problem. I wouldn't be able to think straight either if my clothes were wet and sticking to my skin. Go home and shower. Then we can go back there this evening or tomorrow at noon. Okay?"

I sighed. "Yeah, I guess you're right."

"One day, I'll record that."

Chuckling, I hit end and went to find Larry. He was sitting at the entrance desk, still eating pizza. The large, almost empty cardboard box sat on his chair, and he was typing something on the keyboard.

"The pizza gets the chair, and you have to stand?" I asked, smirking.

"I can't sit for long. By the way, Milly told me your dad is Thomas Harper."

My brow creased. "Why and when did that come up?"

"When we were at the storage unit, we were chit-chatting about antiques. She showed me some pics of your dad's rarest pieces."

"You're a history buff, too?"

"I couldn't care less about historical anything. But I know Milly's passionate about that kind of stuff, so I brought the subject up. Anyway, did you know your dad works for the organization that owns the fairgrounds?"

"New England Exposition owns this property?"

"Yeah. I figured you might want to know since you seem to be interested in this place in regard to your investigation. They have access to our systems."

"You are just overflowing with crucial information today. Thank you, Larry."

He winked. "That's Hairy Larry to you, missy."

I laughed. "Why do you let people call you Hairy Larry?"

"It was either accept the accurate nickname or shave three hours a day. And I'd have to hire someone to do the back of me. No, thank you."

I bit my lower lip, trying not to cringe. "Thanks again. Hairy Larry."

"You're welcome, pretty rat."

I shook my head. "No."

"No? I thought I'd made up a cute nickname for you. Well, good luck, Olivia. If anyone can solve this case, it's you."

24

THE NEXT MORNING, I woke up to the realization that yesterday I may have been diving headfirst down a rabbit hole. With all the evidence someone was handing over, why was I focusing on fairground employees and the key used to open the storage unit? Today, I'd take a different direction and pay a visit to the evidence room.

Not finding Fred in his office, I made a beeline to the break room and found him munching on an apple turnover.

"Good morning, kiddo."

Taking a seat, I crossed my arms. "Good morning, sweet tooth."

"What can I say? Treats keep me sweet," he said, chewing.

I laughed. "Might want to try something else. It's not working."

"How did your fairground visit go?"

"It doesn't matter. I'm changing my strategy for now."

"I think the visit paid off. Unless Larry sucks at reading handwriting. Guess we'll wait and find out what my guy says about the note. I'll get his report today."

"How do you know...do you and Ethan talk every morning?"

"No. Larry called me last night. He's all excited about helping out and wanted to tell me himself."

"I'm not surprised. If it weren't for all his hair, pride would have been oozing out of every pore on his body."

He made a sour expression. "You trying to ruin my appetite?"

I smiled sheepishly. "It surprised me to learn he's the HR guy at the fairgrounds."

"Hairy Larry and I go back many years. He's a good guy. Has a huge crush on Milly."

"What single guy doesn't?"

"Is she still dating what's-his-name?"

"I don't know who what's-his-name is, but she's dating a friend of Ethan's. His name is Norman."

Fred stood and dusted the crumbs from his crisply ironed uniform.

"You're the only detective I know who wears a police uniform," I stated. "Why?"

"Two reasons: to exude my authority, and I don't have to pick out something to wear."

"Should have known that," I said, standing. "I'd like to visit the evidence room if it's a good time."

"Now is as good a time as any," he said, leading the way.

As we approached a heavy metal door marked "Evidence Room," Fred produced a keyring that jingled with an assortment of keys. With a deft twist, he unlocked the door and swung it open, revealing a brightly lit room filled with shelves, boxes, and evidence bags. The scent of paper, ink, and a hint of metallic greeted my senses.

"Welcome to our labyrinth of secrets," Fred kidded. "It's been a long time since you've been in here."

Nodding, I stepped inside. My eyes swept over the rows of shelves, each holding an array of neatly labeled evidence containers, ranging from small envelopes to large, sealed boxes.

Fred took me to a table in the center of the room, where a few opened boxes displayed their contents.

I set my laptop bag down and peered inside.

"It'd be nice if these items talked," Fred said. "The platter did give us a brief message, though. The artist etched letters on the back. We barely made them out." He pointed with his gloved finger. "SH. The examiner figured the letters to be an initial monogram."

"Or perhaps they stand for Sparrow Haven."

"Yeah. Come to find out, it does. Anyway, we tracked down the silver artisan who crafted the platter."

"Who was the artist?"

"An eighty-year-old woman named Meredith Givens. She remembered this piece and told us she'd crafted the platter twenty-five years ago."

"Wow. Why does she remember this platter so vividly?"

"She crafted the platter to be a wedding gift from a groom to his bride. And the design of the ancient tree on the front side of it was based on the place he proposed to her. Ms. Givens thought the groom's idea was one of the most romantic gift ideas ever."

"Did she give you the groom's name?"

"Nope. That's where we hit a dead end. Meredith remembers her pieces, but she's not so good at remembering clients' names."

"I'd like to speak with Ms. Givens," I said. "You know every inch of this town. Have an idea where I can find the tree depicted on the platter?"

He grunted. "You're kidding, right? Sparrow Haven is loaded with hundred-year-old trees."

I shook my head. "This tree is unusual. Look at this prominent branch." I pointed at it. "See how this one arches toward the ground, while the others arch toward the sky?"

He chuckled. "I wish you all the luck tracking down a tree. What's even the point?"

I rolled my eyes. "Fred. This groom is a die-hard romantic. There is a decent chance they engraved their initials on the trunk of that tree."

His brow arched. "I wouldn't know anything about romantic notions. But I think you've come up with a good idea after all. Maybe check with Robert Mosely. He's a local landscape photographer."

"Good idea," I said, feeling infused with inspiration for the first time since working this case.

Fred chuckled. "I've been waiting to see that excited look in your eyes, kiddo. You'll find Meredith's place a few miles down Meadow Lane off of highway seventy-six. You'll know it when you see it."

***

Because of the late morning hour, I'd have to wait to make the trip to Meadow Lane. Before opening the library, I performed one of my daily duties that always seemed to set the tone for the day. I meticulously arranged the books on the front display shelves, ensuring they were perfectly aligned and that each cover faced out, inviting readers with their tantalizing titles and captivating cover art.

Today, as I engaged in this simple task, my heart raced a bit faster than usual. I could hardly focus on the books as my thoughts kept drifting to the lunchtime visit.

After opening, I kept glancing at the grandfather clock between assisting members. Finally, the clock chimed noon, so I gathered my things and headed to my car.

As I turned onto Meadow Lane twenty minutes later, the scenery transformed into a picturesque, winding road. The lush landscape hosting quaint cottages looked as though someone had plucked it from the pages of a storybook. Tall trees created a lush canopy over-head, filtering dappled sunlight onto the road.

Fred was right. It was easy to spot Meredith's home. On the left side of the lane, nestled amidst a colorful array of blossoming gardens, whimsical, silver-made artifacts spotted Meredith's charming cottage. The cottage's façade was adorned with climbing vines, and a white picket fence encircled a neatly kept yard.

Meredith, who was hunched over pruning a rose bush, straightened and waved as if she'd been expecting me. She had a slender frame, and she'd pulled her silver hair into a bun, which shimmered in the sunlight.

Approaching her with a smile, I noted a radiance in her presence. Her blue eyes sparkled as she reached for my hand.

"I was hoping you'd stop by, Olivia."

"How did you know to expect me, Ms. Givens?"

She batted a fly from her floral apron. "Call me Meredith. Well, I figured my platter must be evidence in the murder case you and Detective O'Malley are trying to solve." Meredith's voice sounded strong and smooth. "Let's have a seat on my porch, shall we? What a beautiful summer day we are having!"

I took the offered seat overlooking the yard. Delicate wind chimes tinkled in the wind. Gleaming silver butterflies, crafted with intricate detail, danced along the fence. And a stone birdbath speckled with silver leaves stood in the center of the yard.

"Meredith, I love your craftsmanship. You're very gifted. What prompted you to become a silver artisan?"

She clasped her hands together and smiled. "Family tradition. My mother and her mother for four generations back fell in love with the art. I work in the same workshop out back as my mother and grand-mother did." She displayed swollen fingers. "I still tinker with small pieces, but with these arthritic hands, my days of crafting complicated pieces are over." She giggled. "But I'm thankful for what I can still do at this old age."

"It shocked me when Detective O'Malley told me you still remembered the platter."

She swatted the air. "Oh, it's an easy one to recall. The old tree is unique, and besides, I'll never forget the love in the groom's eyes." She looked dreamily in the distance. "He brought me a lovely photo of the tree and told me he'd proposed to his honey beneath it. He said the tree had become a special meeting place for them."

It was a long shot, but I had to ask. "Did this young man happen to mention where the tree is located in town?"

Meredith's eyes lit up. "Yes, actually. He said the tree stands along a nearby river." She sighed. "I'm not too good at recalling any kind of name, though." She snapped. "But he said it was the perfect spot because of the breathtaking view." She nodded. "I remember something about an old stone bridge."

My breath hitched, knowing I now had something to go by. And Sparrow Haven only had a handful of rivers.

"Meredith, why do you etch S.H. into your art? Instead of your name or initials?"

She wagged her pointer finger back and forth. "The women in my family believe doing so would be vain. And Sparrow Haven has been the source of our inspiration. Therefore, the village receives the credit."

"Our village is beautiful." I glanced at my phone. "I need to get going but thank you for talking with me today."

Her hand flew to her mouth. "Oh dear, I forgot to offer you a beverage. I'm afraid my age is starting to catch up with me. I'm sorry. Would you like—"

I wanted to hug this woman. "No, thank you. I hope I'm as beautiful and sharp as you are when I'm eighty, Meredith."

She smiled. "Well, with compliments like that, I hope you return often to visit."

I returned the smile. "I'd be happy to stop by again."

She rubbed her hands together. "Oh, good. Stop by anytime." She winked. "Now, go find that old tree, Olivia."

I laughed. "I plan on it."

"Would you mind sending me a picture of the tree? I'd love to see how the old oak looks after twenty-five years."

"Sure," I said, before storing her number in my phone.

25

— . —

I DROVE A BIT down the road and then pulled to the side to look up the photographer Fred had mentioned.

As luck would have it, Robert knew exactly which stone bridge Meredith had mentioned. With hopes high, I headed to Willow Brook Creek in search of the Riverbend Bridge. According to Google maps, I'd arrive at my destination in sixteen minutes.

I parked my car on the side of the road, my eyes widening with a sense of wonder and anticipation. Willow Brook Creek stretched out before me, a ribbon of glistening water meandering gracefully along the edge of town. The afternoon sunbathed the landscape in a warm glow, and the babbling of the creek filled the air with a soothing melody.

Before me stood the Riverbend Bridge, a lovely stone structure arching over the creek's gentle waters. Its aged stones bore the marks of time, weathered and worn. Moss clung to the sides like nature's tapestry, adding a touch of rustic charm to the scene.

The gravel crunched beneath my shoes as I inhaled the earthy scent of the creek. The soft rustle of leaves in the nearby willow trees added a serene backdrop to the moment.

As I reached the arch of the bridge, I paused to take in the timeless beauty. I let my gaze wander further downstream, and there it was—the majestic oak tree that had stood sentinel for generations.

I ran to the clearing of velvety grass beneath the one downward branch. My fingers lightly brushed against the rugged bark, searching for what I'd hoped to find.

And I did. A pair of initials, interlocked in a heart, had been lovingly carved into the trunk. SS + NS.

"N.S. Nancy Silverton," I whispered.

My mouth dropped open. S.S. Could that stand for Seth Silverton. Or S could stand for his dad's name, but I wasn't sure what that was. I remembered Seth saying his middle name was Sean. Either way, Nancy had named her son after his father. But Seth had said his dad ran away just after he was born. So, why would she name her son after a husband who had abandoned them?

Circling around to the other side of the massive trunk, I found they'd also carved two animals. The skilled carving portrayed some kind of bird, a hawk I believed, from its sharp, hooked beak and its dominant talons. They'd also carved a detailed butterfly below the bird, with etched stripes and dotted indentions along the wings.

I anxiously pulled my cell phone from my pocket, took close-ups of the carvings on each side of the trunk, and then called Fred, my hands shaking with the thrill of my findings.

"Hey, kiddo. I was just about to call you. Larry was right. My guy is ninety-seven percent sure a woman wrote the note to Richard."

My heart pounded against my ribs. "Nancy Silverton. The platter belongs to Chef Nancy Silverton."

"How sure are you?"

"I'm fairly certain. I believe her son, Seth Silverton, killed Victoria."

"What?"

"Nancy found out Seth poisoned Victoria, and she doesn't want her son to get away with the murder. Nancy couldn't bring herself to turn in her son, so she planted evidence as clues instead. Just as you thought...so we could connect the dots."

"Go on."

"And I think Ethan was right about the killer following me. I think he saw me find the evidence in the storage unit. When Seth spoke with me at the dog park, he knew what his mom was up to. By telling me his mom still hated Victoria, I think Seth was hoping we'd arrest her, based on motive, lies, and her part in making the chowder. Then he'd get away with it."

"Why would Seth kill Victoria?"

"I don't know. Maybe Seth killed her to avenge his mom, thinking she'd be grateful to him. But instead, Nancy turned against him."

I could hear Fred getting in his patrol car. "Can you place Seth at the crime scene?"

"Yes. Seth told me he was at the fair with some friends, and Larry can verify the ticket purchase if he tries changing his story. Or Larry can pull the camera footage from the ticket stand."

"I'm going now to bring them into custody. It's possible they were both in on it, and Nancy got too cocky, and started playing games."

"My gut says otherwise, but that's still a good idea. I'll meet you at the station."

I ended the call, ready to call Milly next.

"Olive, tell me you have good news."

It amazed me how we always had this twin-like connection.

"Fred is on his way to make two arrests as we speak. Nancy Silverton and her son, Seth Silverton."

"What? Oh my gosh!"

"Right? Hey, you know Nancy pretty well, right?"

"Yes. But I didn't think she'd ever kill someone."

"We don't have all the answers yet. But I wanted to ask you something. Why did Nancy's husband leave her right after she had Seth?"

"Huh? Who told you Sean left them?"

"Seth did."

"Why would he lie about something like that? Sean Silverton died in a car crash."

Surprised, I paused to soak in this information. "Um. Okay. What is Nancy and Seth's relationship like?"

"I'd say they are close, but Seth has always been the angry sort. She's taken him to countless psychiatrists trying to fix him through the years."

"Fix what?"

"I don't think doctors have diagnosed Seth with anything in particular. Nancy thinks Seth is angry at God for taking his dad away from them. Major anger issues."

***

I watched with a mixture of sadness and relief as Fred and his partner escorted the suspects into the station.

Nancy's eyes overflowed with tears. She was protesting her innocence, her voice quivering with emotion as she pleaded for understanding.

Seth, on the other hand, remained silent, his eyes darting between his mother and the detectives, his red-faced anger penetrating the air.

I walked in as Fred read the suspects their rights once more, emphasizing their right to remain silent.

Fred led them to a small, sterile-looking interview room. The harsh fluorescent lights cast a stark, unforgiving glare. I followed them, my heart heavy with the weight of the situation.

Fred motioned for me to take a seat next to him. The mother and son were seated across from us. Fred assured them of a fair trial and the importance of cooperating. Nancy nodded, her eyes still brimming with tears, while Seth's face was void of emotion. Fred's partner remained standing at the door with a case folder containing documents and photographs.

Fred just came out and asked the big question. "Nancy, did you poison Victoria Thorne?"

Nancy began sobbing, her shoulders shaking as she spoke. "No. I didn't. But I did plant the evidence. I wrote one note to Richard, and another I typed to Olivia, written as the killer," she said, glancing at me. "I have a key to the storage unit from last year's tasting. After finding the mortar and pestle, I gave the evidence to you on a silver platter. Literally. I knew one of you would trace the platter back to the oak tree. I also know my son illegally bought a copperhead, and he used the venomous snake to threaten Olivia."

"Who brought the box to my library?" I asked, remembering a woman delivered it.

Nancy shrugged and looked at her son.

"What does it matter? The chick didn't know what was inside, anyway."

Nancy sighed. "Seth has never been an easy child."

A small tattoo on the inside of Nancy's lower arm caught my attention. It was of a hawk and a butterfly encircled in intertwined rings. Her and Sean's spirit animals, perhaps?

I jumped when Seth pounded the table with fisted hands. "Poisoning Victoria was my mother's idea." He shot her a glare. "I did what you wanted. And then you rat me out?"

Nancy shook her head. "What are you talking about?"

"A few months back, you said you ought to poison the chowder after finding out Victoria would be the tasting judge."

Her brow creased. "I was kidding, Seth. And you know it. I laughed when I made the ridiculous comment. Never in my wildest nightmares did I think you would poison her."

He cursed. "You told me to get hemlock, to crush the seeds, and to pour the powder into the chowder once you all went to the storage unit for supplies. I was simply doing what I was told, Mother."

Nancy's mouth dropped open. "How can you sit there and make up lies about me after all I've done for you?" She turned to us. "I swear, not a word of what Seth just said is true. Everyone knows I resented Victoria, but I never wished her harm. Knowing what it's like to lose a spouse, I'd never wish it on my worst enemy."

Seth sneered. "It's your fault you're a widow. If you hadn't gotten into that fight, dad wouldn't have left the house and drove drunk."

Nancy buried her face in her hands. "I should have never told you that part. All couples feud, Seth. I told Sean not to leave, but he didn't listen."

"Nancy, would you be willing to take a polygraph test?" Fred asked.

Nancy's nodded. "Yes. I'll take the test right now if you want."

Seth groaned. "I cannot believe you turned in your own son. I thought you would be proud of me."

Her voice cracked. "You took a life. You made Richard Thorne a widower. Seth, you need to face the consequences, and you need to get help. I hope you get both in prison. What I am doing is called tough love."

And then Seth gave her a few choice words a son should never say to a mom. My stomach soured as Nancy cringed against the hurt.

The utter devastation on Nancy's face broke my heart, and I excused myself before the first tear fell.

Fred came out and hugged me. "I'm proud of you, kiddo. This case was tough, especially with Milly being a prime suspect. You did real good."

"Thanks, Fred. I need to get out of here. I'll see you later."

I strolled out of the station and got in my car. Allowing all the emotions from this case to finally settle on my chest, I had a good cry of relief.

Somehow, amidst the tears, I found myself in Milly's driveway. After our phone conversation, her parents and Richard must have come over. They all flooded out the front door and embraced me in one big group hug. There wasn't a dry eye to be found.

Epilogue

The last day of the county fair dawned with a sense of anticipation in the air. It had been a whirlwind couple of weeks, filled with the twists and turns of the murder case that had captivated our small New England town. But today, the sun broke through the partly clouded sky, promising a day of joy and relief as we closed another chapter of our lives.

My ever-supportive boyfriend was by my side, his hand intertwined with mine. Milly and Norman joined us as we made our way to the fairgrounds' entrance. Laughter and the cheerful hum of carnival rides filled the air as we approached the colorful chaos.

We started with the games, trying our luck at ring toss and darts, the sound of clinking of bottles and the cheers of winners creating a festive mood. The taste of sweet victory mingled with the scent of fried dough, which we indulged in without a second thought.

As evening descended, the fairgrounds transformed into a wonderland of moving lights. The Ferris wheel stood tall against the darkening sky, its colorful bulbs illuminating the night like a beacon of joy.

I spotted Ben Fields inside his concession stand assisting a young mother with her toddler son.

"Want to go say hello?" Ethan asked.

"Sure."

He winked. "Just don't go inside this time."

"Ha-ha."

"Norman and I want a slushy," Milly said, linking her arm through his. "Let's meet back up at the Ferris wheel?"

"Sounds good," Ethan said.

As I waited in line, I watched as Norman and Milly talked and laughed as they strolled away. "I've not seen her this happy in a long time," I said, smiling. "They go well together."

"Yeah, the blind date was a rough start, so I'm relieved they ended up clicking."

I laughed. "I'll say. Milly straight said the date was a mistake. I thought for sure their relationship was over before it began."

Ben rested his elbows on the window panel. "Hey, Olivia. Ethan. Finally at the fair for fun? What can I get you?"

Ethan smiled. "That's right. The popcorn smells good. We'll take a bag and two lemonades."

"Anything else?" he asked, glancing at me.

"That'll do. How have you been?"

"Hanging in there. After I close shop tonight, I'm headed out of town for good. Just me, myself, and I."

No surprise there, I thought. "Where are you moving to?"

"No destination. I'll drive south until the area feels right. Might end up in Florida. Who knows."

Ethan handed over his card. "Well, we wish you the best."

He nodded. "You're a nice gal, Olivia. And I'm sorry for throwing a messy wrench into your case. Congrats on solving the case."

"Thank you. But I had a lot of help," I added, nudging Ethan.

We took a seat at a nearby table, crunching on buttery popcorn and sipping the sweet-tart lemonade.

"After talking to Ben, I realized something," Ethan said, tossing a kernel into his mouth. "Have you ever worked an investigation with so many suspects pointing fingers at one another? And all the way up to the very end?"

"You're right. And then being handed the murder weapon on a silver platter," I said, laughing. "I have to give Nancy credit; the platter was creative and brilliant. It took me straight to the source."

Ethan nodded. "You are the one who deserves credit. I'm proud of your work, Olivia.

I shrugged. "Thanks, but all I did was follow the evidence trail back to the old tree."

He placed his arm around my shoulders. "And that was your idea, honey. Will you take me to the oak tree tomorrow? I'd like to see this epic oak and the old bridge."

I took a sip. "Sure. I forgot to get a picture of the tree, anyway. And the place is peaceful and beautiful. I can see why Sean chose the spot to propose to Nancy."

"Why do you want a picture of the tree? For your sleuth portfolio?"

"Aren't you a funny guy this evening? I told Meredith Givens I'd send her a pic, anyway."

"That's cool. An eighty-year-old techy lady."

"She is super cool. I told her I'd come visit from time to time."

By the time Milly and Norman made their way back, we were all done with our snack and beverages.

Our excitement grew as we boarded the brightly colored gondolas of the Ferris wheel, and with a gentle jolt, we began our ascent. The world spread out before us. The fairground below turned into a colorful, light-filled landscape of activity as the cool night breeze swirled around us.

As we reached the highest point of the Ferris wheel, we paused, suspended between heaven and earth. The hanging position turned into a moment of pure serenity, a breath of respite after the storm.

"Hey, Olive," Milly called a few feet behind us."

"What?"

"I'll be staying the night with you and Barkley."

"I know," I said, knowing Milly was dying to hear about the details of our investigation and how all the events played out from beginning to end. I'd filled Richard in on everything last night by himself out of respect for his loss. The story was difficult for him to hear, but in the end, I saw the beginning of closure in his eyes. The moment filled my heart with peaceful contentment, knowing justice had prevailed.

"Olive, let's hope going forward I never have to stay out of an investigation again. It sucked not being able to help my famous sleuth bestie."

"Um, I totally agree. Please don't ever become a suspect again."

"I'll do my best," she said, laughing.

During the rest of the ride, I leaned into the warmth of Ethan and pondered over the intricate web of human emotions, awaiting another mystery in Sparrow Haven.

For me, the fair became a symbol of closure, a testament to the resilience of our town and the enduring bonds of friendship and love.

***

If you loved the twists and turns of this adventure with Olivia, be sure to check another of her cases, and see how Olivia met Ethan in Mystery at the Lighthouse.

This is what readers are saying:

"This is a wonderful cozy mystery book that you can't put down once you begin. With its twists and turns and a little humor along the way, you will definitely want to keep turning pages until the end."

"If you love a suspenseful mystery that takes you on a journey to past secrets that carry on to the present, then you will love this book. I read it in one sitting, which I rarely do."

Here is a Sneak Peek

"I'm headed your way, Milly," I said into my cell phone urgently. "Are any of the buildings damaged?" My lifelong BFF cared about Sparrow Haven just as much as I did. A nasty squall had swept through our village during the night, with gusts just a notch below the weather station, deeming it worthy of a name.

"I haven't spotted any severe damage so far," Amelia answered. "I'll meet you at the library in ten. Is it a tea or coffee kind of day?"

"Coffee for sure. Pumpkin spice please." Before hitting end, I added, "Might as well make Fred a cup, too. You know how he gets after a storm."

I took the next left onto White Pine Avenue. The normally calm morning atmosphere was replaced with villagers bustling about, sweeping driveways and throwing branches and debris into piles.

I frowned as little Tommy stood crying at the foot of his wrecked fort. The boy wiped his face on his sleeve as his dad consoled him.

Pulling my silver Volkswagen into my usual spot on the corner of Main and Blossom, I grabbed my leather tote and headed to the library at a fast clip. Never too busy to appreciate the view, I admired the historical charm of the Victorian architecture as if it were the first time

I had passed through. I'd lived in this coastal New England village all of my thirty-three years, alongside Amelia. As an only child, Milly was the closest thing to a sister I'd ever had.

Sure enough, standing outside the library on the large, slabbed sidewalk was Detective Fredrick O'Malley. Some didn't know this, but under the police officer's tough exterior, there was a compassionate and empathetic heart. Of course, Fred had threatened to beat me within an inch of my life if I ever told anyone. I'd had a stomach-aching laugh over it too because Fred wouldn't hurt a bee if it stung him on the rump.

I stepped over to Milly and took the cup of coffee she held out to me. "Thank you, Milly." I took a sip. "You'd be an angel if it weren't for you teasing all the men with those wicked heels of yours," I added with a wink.

She stuck her tongue out. "And don't you look lovely today, Olive." (She was the only one allowed to call me that. I'd given up telling her to stop in kindergarten.)

Smiling, I glanced at myself in the window behind her. I didn't consider myself beautiful like Milly, but I was content enough with the way my wavy blonde hair framed my heart-shaped face.

Fred bent over the base of a freshly painted lamp post to retrieve a piece of cardboard. "Nice of you to arrive after we've cleaned up, Olivia Harper," he gruffly stated.

I sent him an overly sweet smile and pointed to the hanging library sign. "You missed one," I chided, pointing at a fallen branch.

Savoring the warm, creamy flavor of fall, I linked my arm through Milly's. "This street never gets old, does it," I said, noticing the way the sun's rays danced across the gray and pink speckled cobblestone street.

Just then, a group of teenagers came rushing down the lane, yelling my name. The tallest of the four was holding something up as if it were a hard-earned trophy.

"Now, what have these kids gotten into this time?" Fred complained, glancing down to ensure his ironed shirt was tucked in straight and tight. He pulled his pants up a notch higher than necessary before placing his hands on his hips. The stance wasn't called for, really. Although a bit grizzled in appearance, the detective's shortly cropped salt-and-pepper hair, deep-set eyes, and strong jawline gave him a naturally stern, imposing presence no matter how he stood.

I tossed my empty cup into the iron waste bin before rubbing my hands together in anticipation. Having become known as the village's amateur sleuth, I was willing to bet my pearl earrings that the teens had another juicy mystery for me to solve. I glanced at Fred, who was casting an amused look my way. He'd known me my entire life and had watched Milly and me grow curious and inquisitive throughout the years. My bestie and I went from embarking on imaginary adventures and mysteries fueled by the stories we'd read and tales told to us by our elders to eventually solving actual cases. At first, the seasoned detective considered us more of a nuisance, but with each passing case we solved, Fred's respect for our passion grew. He'd even provided us with insight to help along the way.

I glanced at Milly, who looked as excited as I felt. She peered closer. "Is that a painting?" she asked, as the teens drew closer.

"Judging by the frame, I'd say it's a good possibility. I keep telling you to get your eyes checked, stubborn girl," I added, giving a light jab with my elbow.

The teens joined us on the sidewalk. "Look what we found, Olivia!" Nathan proudly announced. "It's a painting. A good one, too," he added, his cheeks turning pink as he shyly regarded me.

"Where did you guys find it?" I asked, reaching for the tarnished frame that appeared to be about the size of a sixteen-by-twenty portrait.

"In the abandoned lighthouse up the coast. The storm last night blew part of the wall right off, revealing a hidden chamber!" Nathan said with bright eyes. "We thought you might be interested in finding out where this came from. Are you?"

"Are you kidding?" I asked. "You had me at hidden chamber. Thanks for bringing this to me, Nathan!"

The teen nodded his head with a giddy smile plastering his face.

Get your copy of Mystery at the Lighthouse.

Made in United States
Troutdale, OR
06/27/2024